INTO THE
TUNNEL OF MURDER

INTO THE TUNNEL OF MURDER

Copyright © 2023 by Mennah Abdalqader.

Book and Cover design by : Mennah Abdalqlaqder
ISBN: 979-8-8533486-5-3

First Edition: July 2023

10 9 8 7 6 5 4 3 2 1

For my Dad, Mum and Brother, the best family ever.

INTO THE

TUNNEL OF MURDER

Mennah Abdalqader

PROLOGUE

It was a dark night. Not ANY dark night. An EVIL dark night, evil was in the air, and it was up to no good. This dark evil night didn't come by itself, oh no. In a dark shed (that nobody really pays attention to) underground, lived a mysterious professor whom only people have heard of, but never seen. He was busy in his laboratory mixing potions and spells; he used the most disgusting things. Human eyeballs, rats, leeches, left over nachos that nobody wanted, bones, cockroaches, an old man's toenail, dandruff, snot and saliva. There was a woman watching him. Well, I think she was a woman, but she looked more like a zombie. With blackish-red eyes and blonde-slick hair and yellow teeth and greenish kind of skin. She tried to hide that by putting face and skin cream. So, if she was ever on a mission, she wouldn't reveal her identity. She watched as he cautiously poured the final potion in a cup and slowly lifted his head and looked at her. She smiled. She knew her boss professor would need her to go on a mission soon.

1
BIG NEWS

"Wake up you lazy lot!" shouted Jess as she started jumping crazily on the bed. Jess was the youngest of the group but the craziest. She was good at lots of things and has this awfully cute voice that makes her sound 5 instead of 10. She can be awfully loud at sometimes, which, gets on people's nerves. "OH MY, JESS! Stop this intense jumping before I snap your neck in half!" this was her sister, Mia. Though sisters, they were complete opposites, Mia was fierce, Jess was not. Jess was babyish, Mia was not. Jess immediately stopped jumping, her sister could be a bit scary sometimes and sometimes a bit of a meanie.

"Sorry Meeeeeeeea!" said Jess.

"What the heck is all that noise?" this, is Harry, who often wakes up <u>AFTER</u> all the noise is made.

"It's the 'Jess and Mia Show' come and watch!" said Cara. She was obsessed with crabs and refers to herself as Cara Crab. The rest of the group were also watching. There was Frank, Leo and Andrew; the rest of the boys. And Tess was the only other girl.

"VERY funny Cara, we need to get ready for breakfast quick before Chips comes and boils us nagging," said Mia jumping off the bed.

CHIPS. It was a word they heard every day. Chips was their boss; they worked at a spy agency called Red Potatoes and Chips was their fierce, scary and shouty boss who was always nagging and shrieking at them.

"YA GUYS! We don't want Chips coming and start **NAGGING US TO DEATH**!" Exclaimed Jess, jumping up and down.

They quickly got off the bed and started getting dressed. They had matching short-sleeve shirts that had the Red Potatoes logo and above it said 'RED POTATOES SPY' and their name.

They all had the same size and fitted most of them perfectly, except Jess, it was very baggy and reached her knees, so you could hardly see her shorts.

They were just about to open the door, until 'SOMEONE' opened it for them- "ARE YOU STILL IN HERE!!??" shrieked a certain someone, "I HAVE *THE GOOD GROUP* ALREADY DOWNSTAIRS EATING! MILLIE- ERR- MISS MUSH CAN'T WAIT FOR YOU LOT ALL DAY" Chips shouted then slammed the door.

The 'Good Group' were another group who were-err- good. But don't get fooled by the word 'good'! Good as in kind, polite, gentle and sweet, THAT kind of good. But they weren't good at spying or missions or anything like that, them and The Terrible Group (the original group) were complete opposites. *THE GOOD GROUP* is made up of Becky, Amy, Hannah, Sally, Thomas, Alfie, Charlie and Max.

They waited a few seconds before Leo opened the door and they went to the cafeteria.

When they got there and lined up to get their food, Miss Millie Mush smiled at them, "You took your time!" she said kindly and then gave a little laugh. Mia was first, (somehow) "Got a bit held up by Chips, you know!" she told her.

"Ah yes, I understand! Typical Chips! Now darling, what will you be having?"

When they all got their breakfast, they took a seat at the dining table. But since they were last, some of them had to sit around the most random people.

Tess was beside Love Texas, Tom Millar and opposite to her was Amy from the good group. Frank was beside Florence First Aid, Hannah Walters and opposite him was Andrew.

Phew! Could have been much worse! he thought.

While they sat and munched and chewed and chatted to everyone around them, Chips suddenly came down with two workers and announced. "Good morning Red Potatoes," she said.

"Goooood morning Chipsssss," everybody droned lazily and sleepily.

"When you are all done your breakfast, MAKE IT SNAPPY! I would like you all to come down to the hall as I have an important announcement to make. EVERYONE. NEEDS. TO. COME! Do I make myself clear?"

"Yesss Chipss," they replied, some of them still half asleep. And with that, Chips walked out.

"PHEW! That was a close call! I thought she came in to complain about my dirty socks being everywhere!" said Harry and everybody laughed.

While everyone was just finishing up, Mia asked Alex Basil (an adult spy who works there), when was the last time everyone was called up to the hall.

"Well, lil' lass I can't be too 'ure but it may 'ave been when you 'ere very lil' indeed!" he chuckled.

Mia sighed, he was no help whatsoever. *Grown-ups!* She thought *well I may soon find out!* And they were led out.

Everybody took a seat and waited for the maybe 'dreaded' announcement Chips was just about to send into their ears.

"**WELCOME TO THE HALL EVERYBODY!**" Chips was shouting loudly because there was about 150 people in the room.

"**I believe it may have been 8 years since our last meeting here, grown-ups you better remember!**"

Alex Basil doesn't! thought Mia and laughed in her head

"**I have some big news to share, tomorrow some of us will have the biggest task EVER in the history of the Red Potatoes. It is hosted by the owner of agencies and spies, Richard Lewis!**"

"**He has decided to invent something UNBELIEVABLE, something so- so I DON'T EVEN KNOW!! Only those who are brave and trustworthy can survive! And us, the Red Potatoes, ARE PARTICIPATING!**"

There was a few silent groans as they didn't think they'd like what was coming.

"**Let me explain; first, to let you know before ANYTHING ELSE, I need to tell you the other agencies participating! Let me see ...**"

She took out a list and said,

"**AGENCIES: Takeaway Timers, Sassy Grannies, The Globs, Marshmallow City, CHOCOLATE WORLD our friends, Rough Cakes, Wannabe Bears, Toilet Nails, Creepy Crawlies, Aliens 'n' America, blah blah blah.....**"

Many agencies later

"**....... AND......**"

Her eyes drooped a little as she said this one,

"**AND SADLY, OUR BIGGEST ENEMIES...... THE RED POETOES!**"

There was a load of different emotions around the hall, a few whispers and gasps and shrieks, you may be thinking 'Why biggest enemies??' well it's because ..... DUN DUNN DUNNNN ..... The Red Poetoes copied their name!!! (If you haven't guessed that already) It's not exactly the same but it's a bit TOO similar, don't you think? Because there's Red 'Potatoes' and Red 'Poetoes' (here is a small guide to pronounce it: You know the way Father Christmas goes HO HO HO it is pronounced like that only a 'p' instead of a 'h' and then the word toes!! So, Poetoes! Easier than you thought, eh?) SO YEAH!

Chips continued her announcement,

"**BE QUIET! <u>ENOUGH</u> TALKING THANK YOU VERY MUCH!!!** * everyone quiets down *

"**RIGHT! Now the task is about killing and spying! Which I know some of you enjoy...... AND SOME OF YOU DON'T! Well, anyway, all these agencies will go into a GIANT TUNNEL, the group picked from each team to go will get a HUGE BED that will be a safe zone and also.... well... a BED!**

You will go out every day for **A MONTH**, to do **KILLING** to anybody not on your team. Kill, hold hostage, even expand your team by getting more members, that's what were here for!"

"Well actually, **NOT EXACTLY!** Inside that tunnel, there is a secret place that has golds and riches and **ALL SORTS!** First team to find it, **WINS**, so actually it's not **JUST** a month you stay there, **OH NO!** It's as long as it takes to find those riches and we're going be there **TO GET THEM FIRST!**"

"To pick who's coming, I have a hat here with everyone's names in it. If you're picked, you pick **SEVEN PEOPLE** to come with you. No matter who you chose, don't worry I'll be there with you!!"

That certainly made a few people feel better, with CHIPS, NOTHING felt impossible!

"**HAT PLEASE, CHOP CHOP!**"

A tall thin man came in with a top hat, and in the top hat were loads of little paper with little NAMES on them!

"**THANK YOU, Harold. Anyway, NOW, HAT TIME!!**"

She held out the hat in one hand and in the other, she put her hand inside the hat, and moved her hand around. Then, she stopped, picked on up, and opened it before saying . . .

"........**TESS GARCIA! NOW TESS! Which seven people are you bringing??**"

Tess swallowed before saying, "I will bring, Mia Badger, Jess Badger, Cara Michaels, Frank Johnson, Leo Brooks, Harry Peters and Andrew Smith!"

The Terrible Group, had no idea how to feel. Only one person knew what to do. Mia. She stood up on her chair and shrieked "YAAAAAAHOOOOO!!" while the others sat there, stunned no idea what to do.

"Well, that is the whole terrible group then! I suppose YOU'LL Be coming WITH me to the tunnel, hope you're excited, folks this is a ONCE IN A LIFE EXPERIENCE! Well thank you for listening, though, actually, you're EXPECTED to listen to me. MISS MUSH! Prepare some of you VERY RARE, COOKIES AND CREAM, as a treat IF we win the RICHES AND WE DON'T DIE!"

"AND, BEFORE you all go I'd like to WARN Harry Peters to STOP getting his DIRTY SOCKS EVERYWHERE I go! Got that Harry??"

Harry nodded and his face went really red. He smiled at the laughing people around him, Cara in particular, who was laughing so much she might fall right off her chair.

"SILENCE PLEASE! Now that's sorted I want you all to get TO BED as that meeting took me ALL DAY TO SAY! Now good sleeping and TERRIBLES, I'll see you tomorrow at 4:30AM!"

2
STOLEN BISCUITS

The Terrible Group went asleep shaking with excitement and fear. They got dressed into their PJs which were also matching 'Red Potatoes' ones. Before he went to sleep, Harry made sure to pick up every last dirty sock he could find! He found one in the toilet which wasn't satisfying. "I am NOT going through another 'Embarrassing Harry Show' especially not in front of the WHOLE entire agency!" said Harry when he came back from his dirty sock hunt (precisely 96 socks found). "It was actually a bit funny when Chips complained about your dirty socks!" said Cara forgetting her 'crab' day dream and joining in their 'sock' chat. "**A BIT**?!!? **A BIT**!!? **A BIT**?!? You were laughing YOUR HEAD RIGHT OFF!!" shrieked Harry, going a bit over the top, "Gee! Sorry Harry, it was just MEGA funny!!" said Cara before she started day dreaming about 'cute crabs' all over again. "**GRRRRR!** I'll get you for this CARA CRABBY BRAIN!!" growled Harry, his face going red like a tomato. "Guys we should really get to bed now," said Tess, trying to lighten the mood, "Tomorrow's the big day!" she cheered.

"YAA JESSY CAN'T WAIT!!!!!!!" Jess, the Absolutely No Joke Is Very Crazy, shouted in excitement "OH MY GOD! BE QUIET the lot of you!" sighed Mia trying to ignore this conversation that made absolutely NO sense. "The next person to speak, I will LITERALLY make their life not worth living!!" whispered Frank dramatically. Then two seconds later he beamed, because they had actually listened to him, AND SHUTED RIGHT UP! "Whatever!" muttered Mia jealously.

When they finally settled in their bed, yes BED, I said <u>BED</u>! ONE SINGLE BED!! Is that what surprises you? Eight people in one bed? I know that's just messed up, but unfortunately, it is true! One hundred percent true! Though, it is a king-size bed! Still – I know - EIGHT PEOPLE! The girls are on one side and the boys on the other, so yeah, sometimes their legs meet and they have a huge kick-fight, but don't get me started on that……. Rightttt…….? Right okay, back to story! They settled in the KING-SIZE bed and had a few small chats between them, want to know details Mr./Miss. Nosy? Here it is:

Tess and Mia chatted about how EXCITED they were for the trip-of-probably-death tomorrow. Cara day - dreamed (or NIGHT dreamed) about a 'Crabs Killer Party' and how she and her heroic gang of crabs won. Jess just lay there sucking her thumb and cuddling her FAVOURITE cuddly cheetah named Mr. Scruffles. Harry fell asleep straight away and had a nightmare about dirty socks in the toilet. Andrew started reading a book called 'How To Survive Something You Don't Want To Do SPY EDITION' while sharing the information to Leo and Frank. Leo and

Frank were chatting about crisps and toes while getting information by Andrew. HOPE YOU HAD FUN GETTING INFORMED!! After they did all that stuff, they all went to sleep and couldn't wait for the morning. (SOME of them couldn't wait) I say they slept but some didn't. HARRY and CARA SUCCESSFULLY fell asleep easily while others were finding it a bit of a struggle. Jess started crying because she didn't want to wake up at 4:30am for some stupid mission. Mia heard her as she had very sharp ears, and whispered "What's the matter?"

"Errrr, Mr. Scruffles' fur is a bit damp and I DON'T LIKE IT!!!" she replied. Mia sighed, even JESS wouldn't cry over that! "Hmmm, I don't think some stupid damp fur is making you cry if I'm being honest!" she said and Jess glared at her sister *what an idiot!* She thought *she thinks she's the LOVELY BIG sister well I ain't telling her nothing!* "I'm just cwying for da sake of cwying, otay? So go away now!" she decided to say in the end. Mia sighed once more, "Sure you are, just shut the baby voice up and you'll be PERFECTLY Fine, OKAY?" What an irritating sister! This WAS Jess's real voice!!!! "BUT THIS IS MY VOICE!!!!!" she whisper-shouted.

"Okay okay, whatever, stop the baby words then, happy?!" of course Jess was not happy! If only Mia had shut up and not spoken to her! What a waste of a page! Even I, the humble narrator agrees! But, oh well, I have to tell you everything!

Anyway, while this 'Jess and Mia' show was happening the boys decided it was a good idea to eat some stolen biscuits from the girls, they hoped Mia and Jess wouldn't notice, especially Jess, she could be quite fierce when it came to stolen Jammie Dodgers! "Mmm-mmm-mmm! Nothing tastes better than a packet of stolen biscuits!" said Leo spraying crumbs everywhere.

"Deffo dude!" agreed Andrew, spraying even more.

"Spot on!" said Harry, spraying EVEN more!

"Well said!" replied Frank spraying WAY too many crumbs even the other boys were disgusted now.

As they were finishing off the last few digestive biscuits, they saw Cara's face right in front of them, and she was looking at the biscuits. "WHAT DO YOU THINK YOU'RE DOING?!!? Those biscuits were EMERGENCY biscuits, us girls saved them up to eat when Old Miss Musho makes something we don't like!! AND we were going to share them, but you've scoffed the whole lot! Everything! Even Jess's jammies!" she whisper-shouted at them. With her big ears, Mia overheard Cara's whisper-shouting (though you don't need big ears to hear Cara's whisper-shouting). "What's up Cara?" she said, but then caught sight of the crumbs and packets all over the place and Cara's face looking directly at them, "Do NOT tell me you just ate all that!" she said as she looked over at Cara's face, Cara just nodded but didn't say anything. "Even the sweets and lemon sherbets and white mice and gummy bears and...." She gasped, "EVEN THE JAMMIE DODGERS?!!?" the boys were starting to get a bit nervous now, was it THAT much of a big deal? What if they told Jess? She would turn into an Angry Jess if she heard this. She and her Mr. Scruffles would RIP their heads off their shoulders if they ate her jammies, and they just did…….

"What's all this noise?" asked Tess appearing from behind them. "Me and Jess were just discussing Jammie Dodgers and when we're going to eat them, but we heard all this noise and wanted to know what in the name of Jammie Dodgers was going on!" she said. Mia and Cara didn't say anything. They just stared at the empty wrappers. Tess followed their gaze and saw the empty packets. She gasped, and soon Jess came and joined them …..

"HIYA PALS!! What's goin' on round here?" she said with a big and cheesy smile, holding Mr. Scruffles in one hand. The boys started to feel an inseey tinseey bit bad, Jammie Dodgers were Jess's favourite thing ever! And they had just eaten every single one of her packets! Jess sensed something was up and asked her 'gang' what was wrong. "We may have a bit of an issue with the sweets…." Said Sweet Tess who was not willing to get the boys into trouble yet. She went up to where everyone was looking and saw … the dreadful sight of sweets and chocolate and BISCUIT wrappers …… "Don't tell me, you nasty smelly boys ate my jammies???" she looked up at the scared 'smelly' boys.

"PLEASE DON'T TELL ME YOU DARED EAT ALL MY POCKET MONEY SAVINGS!!!!!!!!!" (yeah, Chips gave them pocket money and she spent hers on sweets).

Her eyes were like fire now, and the boys were scared out of their wits. "Ok we won't..." Leo DARED whispered. Like her sister, she had sharp ears. "ARE YOU MESSING WITH ME??!!" she glared at where he was sitting and went up to him. "DID YOU ACTUALLY JUST DARE SAY THAT AFTER YOU'VE EATEN ALL MY POCKET MONEY EARNINGS?!!?" she spat, clearly mad and utterly disgusted with all four boys. She raised her hand and was just about to punch them with good, old Mr. Scruffles until the door opened, "DID YOU DARE STAY UP TILL ONE O'CLOCK AND THINK YOU WOULD GET AWAY WITH IT??!!" It was Chips, as you can guess, and she wasn't very happy. They all froze mid-air and stared at Chips. "GET TO BED **RIGHT NOW** BEFORE I KILL YOU ALL!! WE'RE GETTING UP AGAIN IN ONLY THREE AND A HALF HOURS!! **SO.GET.TO.BED**!!!" she screamed. They immediately got in their positions and pretended to fall asleep. Then they heard a little voice, "We are sorry, Chips. But we can't seem to fall asleep by all the shouting!" it was Hannah from the GOODY GOOD GROUP. "Oh, I'm very sorry dear, I shall stop shouting, get to bed now!" she smiled, then she looked back at the IRRITATING boys and girls and glared at them. Then slammed the door shut. "What a lucky escape!" said Harry.

"You bet!" agreed Leo.

"We were just about to get a great whippin' by an Angry Jess!" exclaimed Frank.

"Until Chips saved us!" added Andrew.

"Will you all stop giggling and whispering like the ugly monkeys you are?! We're still going to get you back for this!" Mia whisper– shouted. The boys were in a good mood from their $LUCKY$ escape, so they decided to shut up for once and listen to Mia. Mia immediately beamed in the darkness *Ha!* She thought *beat THAT Frank! I can make people listen to me EASILY!* And they all fell asleep, dreaming their own magical dreams (or nightmares of an Angry Jess riot or dirty socks in the toilet).

3
CRAZY SIGHTS

THUMP Mia hit the ground like a giant wrecking - ball. Mia always fell off the bed when it was time to get up. Nobody knew how or why, but it always woke them up. The rest of the group sat up quickly and Frank looked at the time. "It's 4:29am! Chips will be banging at our door any minute now!" indeed he was right, Chips would be sure to give them a great nagging if she found them not ready. Harry suddenly sat up and looked like he'd seen a giant donkey attacking his underpants. "IM SORRY!! NO MORE DIRTY SOCKS!!!!!!!" he screamed. "What the heck Harry!!? We don't have time for dirty socks! Chips will come and shriek at us if we don't get ready in the next thirty secondssss," Mia said, still vey lazy and sleepy like the rest of them. They dragged their feet over to the clothes closet and got their clothes, but as they were lazy and droopy, they didn't look at the names of the shirts and picked the most RANDOM ones. "Hayy Tessss, why doesss yourr shirttt say Annndrew Sssmithh??" said Frank exaggerating a bit. She looked down, "Whoops!" she said and started to take it off. "Oh guys! We don't have time! Chipss will kill uss!" said a very sleepy Cara who was fighting to stay awake. And she was right, as everyone was taking off the shirts there was a VERY, and I mean VERY, loud

BANG

And right in the doorway was standing a very angry Chips. "YOU LOT ARE JUST EMBARRASING! THE COACH IS WAITING OUTSIDE AND YOU'RE- TAKING OFF YOUR SHIRTS??!! WHAT KIND OF OFF - THE SCALE MADNESS IS THAT!!? JUST GET MOVING!" she shouted, highly irritated by this room of 'terribles'. "SORRY CHIPS!! It's just we wore the wrong shirts, by mistake!" said Jess, hoping that would lighten her mood. "NOT GOOD ENOUGH, AND I SAID GET MOVING!" she shrieked, even louder this time. Jess closed her eyes, as spit was getting all over her face, and she quickly swapped shirts with Leo while everyone else got changed. After another two minutes, they finished getting dressed and everyone was in their right clothes, so they went down for a quick breakfast before they headed off.

"What are you having then, dear?" Miss Mush said. She was in a bit of a bad mood, because she had been woken up at 4:30am just to make some stupid breakfast for a bunch of kids.

"Just cheerios please Mush," swaggered Frank, showing off his hair that he had just put gel on before they left. *Kids these days!* Thought Miss Mush *acting rotten and trying to act cool and treat us adults like old – fashioned dirt! What a cheek!* After she had gone through all of the 'rotten' children (including a hot chocolate for Chips), she closed the cafeteria and jumped onto her bed like a dolphin somersaulting into the sea. They quickly ate their breakfast in a rush, unable to enjoy every mouthful. It didn't help with Chips screaming in the back ground for them to hurry up. Not a very good breakfast, don't you think?!

As they were eating, they started waking up a bit more. They didn't feel as lazy or sleepy as before, which was a good sign, right? Or was it? If they were practically asleep would they have seen the **UNBELIEVABLE** and **SO – SO THEY DIDN'T KNOW** thing that was right in front of their very own eyes? Would've they? Are you interested? No? Oh well, you better listen anyway:

As they were finishing off the last few mouthfuls, Chips randomly said "I'll be right back, I just need to pack one more thing." And she disappeared upstairs. It gave them a chance to relax without the screaming in the background going on. "*P*eaceeeeeee!" said Tess closing her eyes. Jess giggled and drooled a bit. But then Mia said, "Be quiet! Especially you Tess! You're the one who got us in this mess!" Then Tess started to feel a bit guilty about it. *Why should I though?* She thought *I can't help it! My luck, okay? You're the one who was SCREAMING your head off in excitement when I picked you! So shut it up, Meanie Mia!* Then Tess felt guilty all over again, it's like a devil took over her body for a second, so she just said

"Sorry!" and put her head down, facing her almost - empty, plate of cheerios and milk.

But then, something happened that DEFINITELY woke them all up. A sight that made their eyes grow big, their jaws drop, their brain explode from intense sightings! It was.....................wait for it.......................nearly there!...............it was........................

DUN DUNNN DUNNNNN! CHIPS! HUH? Has she gone out of her mind? Chips is something they see every day! No - But this Chips was DANCING wearing a... DRESS with a MOP! And a black CAT trailing behind her, wearing a pair of neon pink SUNGLASSES! And on top of her head was a radio playing a song from the 1990s perhaps, or 1890s or 1790s! She was dancing around without a care in the world, with the mop like it was a prince or something!

The Terrible Group just sat there absolutely STUNNED their mouths wide open in shock. The song stopped and then came the familiar "My Heart Will Go On" from the *titanic*. Then Chips abandoned Mr. Mop and started dancing with the CAT. They danced slowly with fake tears in their eyes. A few seconds later it changed to a heavy music rock band and Chips randomly said "HIT IT TIPTOES!" and the cat randomly took out an electric guitar and started dancing with Chips like as if they were Metal Music Celebrities. Jess decided to go ask Florence First Aid what was wrong with Chips.

"Ahh," said Florence, after Jess told her what happened. "Chips has this medical thing that if she heard any of her favourite songs, she would go mad and forget the world! Something might've accidently pressed the radio and started the music so she started going mad! Just stop the music and she'll be fine! Oh, and this medical thing also comes with a phobia of pillows!" which explained why Chips hated pillows so much. So Jess went back downstairs and told her 'gang' what Florence told her. "Perfect! Now, who's gonna actually stop the music?" Cara asked.

"How about a vote?" Tess suggested.

"Sure!" said Leo.

"Yeah!"

"Agreed!"

"Sounds fair!"

"OKAY!!!!!"

"Ummmmm?"

"Ok then! Votes for Andrew?" said Mia and no hands go up.

"YES!!!" he said.

"Righht. Votes for Leo?" one hand goes up, it's Jess's.

"BECAUSE YOU STOLE MY JAMMIES!" she shouted.

"HEY!" he complained.

"SHUSH! Now, votes for Frank?" two hands, its Cara's and Mia's.

"BRO WHAT!!" he also complains.

"BE QUIET! Anyway, votes for Harry?" one hand, its Frank's. "Sorry mate! It's just that your dirty socks are just always in my face, so yeah!"

"GRRRRRRRRRRRRR!" Harry growled.

"I SAID. BE. QUIET. Now, votes for Tess?" no hands, she smiled gratefully.

"HUMPHH. Okay, votes for Cara?" one hand, its Harry's, of course. "PAY BACK FOR LAUGHING AT ME!!" he shouted pointing at her. "Shut up!!" she also complained.

"SILENCE! Now. Votes for Jess?" One hand again, its Leo's.

"BECAUSE YOUR JAMMIE DODGERS TASTED A BIT OUT-OF-DATE!" he shouted and then starts laughing for no reason.

"I WILL SUE YOU IF YOU DON'T SHUT UP! Anyway, votes for me?" two hands, Andrew and Tess.

"Bro what?! What have I ever done to you?" Andrew just shrugged and Tess said "I hadn't voted for anybody so I had to vote for you!" and Mia glared at her.

"Sadly, it's a tie between me and Frank so you're going to have to vote again but only for one of us now! So, votes for me?" four hands go up, it's the boys. *Phew!* Thought Mia *half and half! I'll just have to sort it out!* But then Jess started giggling uncontrollably, and slowly put her hand up. "JESS I <u>WILL</u> GET YOU FOR THIS!" shrieked Mia, as she just realized that she was gonna have to turn off the radio. And once she does, Chips will stop dancing. Stare at Mia. And start shrieking at her. Didn't sound too good to Mia. She folded her arms and glared at them, especially Jess, who simply giggled and shrugged as if to say *"It's nothing personal!"* Mia gritted her teeth at her

TERRIBLE sister, and started waking in the direction Chips was dancing madly.

4
A MYSTEROUS LADY

Chips was still dancing with Black Cat when Mia went up to her, but this time they both had sunglasses, mini handbags, a dress on and flying notes and dollars were falling on top of them. They were listening (or dancing) to an old California song from the 1970s, a fashion song to be precise. They were walking around the kitchen like it was a Cat Walk, and Mia started feeling very nervous about Chips' reaction when she turned the old, dusty radio off. What about Black Cat? Would she attack her? Would Chips throw Mia out the window? Her mind was spinning as she walked up to them, and then found herself standing right in front of them. "Errr - excuse me to bother – but – err - I need to turn this radio off - err - yeh - heh." And she slowly moved her shivery hand forward and quickly turned OFF the radio. She closed her eyes and waited for Chips' voice to start screaming at her, but, it didn't happen! She slowly opened her eyes, to see Chips staring back at her. Then out of nowhere she said "I needed that," and looked at her watch that said 4:46am.

"OH NO! We are going to be **AN HOUR LATE** or something AND ITS ALL YOUR FAULT!! STUPID LITTLE *SLOW COACHES*!!" she shrieked at them, not noticing she was still in her dress. The Terrible Group sighed; it wasn't their fault Chips was dancing like an old hooligan! But they delt with it and picked up their bags, ready to go. Chips disappeared into the bathroom and came back in with her usual black outfit. **It was so black. Blacker than coal. Blacker than black nothingness. Blacker than blackest black you will ever come across.**

Enough blacks now! She came out, with her usual clothes and suitcases, god knows what was actually in them. Sweets? Jess thought. Weapons? Mia guessed. Crabs? Cara was thinking. Stolen biscuits? Thought Leo. A radio to dance with? Frank suggested. With a black cat? Added Harry into Frank's thoughts. (Please don't ask me if they can mind read or something, because seriously, you don't even want to know).

They put on their MATCHING Red Potatoes shoes. And slowly approached the coach with a very angry bus driver in it. "OI MATE! 20 MINUTES 'ATE?! WHAT WERE YOU DOIN' IN 'ERE? DANCING?" he shouted as they approached him. *Good guess!* Thought Mia with a small smirk. "WELL, WHATTA YOU EXPECT? 4:30 ON THE DOT? IMPATIENT LITTLE BUS GOODERS!" Chips shouted back, and they all hurried onto the coach before he changed his mind about taking them.

Jess sat beside Tess, behind was Leo and Harry, opposite was Mia and Cara, in front was Andrew and Frank, behind Leo was Chips and opposite Chips was Sinister. Smith (he's actually called Mr. Smith but all the children call him Sinister. Smith. Maybe because he is). He is a staff at Red Potatoes who went into different agencies and hacked through their computers and killed people if necessary. He was the staff picked to go on the mission with them. You couldn't tell how he was feeling, as his face always stays expressionless.

They were due in the tunnel by 5:30, so they only had 40 minutes left, they tried to enjoy their thirty minute trip as much as possible, by sharing sweets (they weren't sure what they were going to eat over there) telling jokes, getting some more sleep (mainly Harry), playing coach games, chatting about how on earth were they going to survive, reading books (only SPY EDITION books were allowed) and staring out the window, which was complete darkness. "PUT A LEG ON IT!" Chips shouted at the poor bus – driver. There was lots of traffic for some reason, even if it was only ten minutes to five AM. "Sorry!" said the poor bus driver. He had just discovered what kind of person Chips was, and didn't dare talk back to her. The trip was very bumpy and everyone just wanted to get off. But then, a random lady wearing a red suit that airplane people wear, came out of nowhere and started handing out drinks and snacks. She had hard-looking skin that had a hint of green but was mostly tan, her hair was a dirty blonde with hints of black in it, her eyes were the most unforgettable black. With a hint of red, too. She started at the front.

"What would you like, darlings?" she asked Frank and Andrew with a smile. She had a soft, smooth voice. Almost too soft and smooth it felt as if it couldn't possibly be real. "Just a packet of Walker's Ready Salted crisps and a cup of orange juice. AND MAKE IT SNAPPY!" Frank replied, irritated he had been called 'darling'.

"A packet of Lunch-Ables and black current juice. RIGHT NOW!" Andrew said, going back to his SPY book. The lady smiled and gave them their orders and said, "That will be £2.49 for you," pointing at Frank, "And £1.89 for you." She said pointing at Andrew.

"WHAT? You have to pay?! What a rip off!" grumbled Frank as they handed over their money.

"Thank you." smiled the lady as she walked over to the next people, which was Jess and Tess.

"That lady was a bit sus!" said Andrew "Handing out snacks on a thirty- minute trip! And she was a bit *too* nice, always smiling!" he added.

"That, is a very good point! Let's check our snacks and see if they have poison in them!" Frank replied. So, they checked to see if there was something UNUSUAL or DIFFERENT about their snacks. "Can you find anything?" asked Andrew.

"Nope! No luck! What about you?" replied Frank with a small sigh. "Nothing here!" Andrew said, "But maybe try and take a bite out of one of your crisps and see what it's like!" So, as Andrew suggested, Frank took a small bite out of a crisp and immediately regretted it. "EWWWWW! It tastes absolutely disgusting! So disgusting, it feels as if it is one thousand years old!" Frank said in disgust.

"Umm - we better warn the others quickly!" said Andrew. They looked back and saw the lady serving

Sinister Smith. As usual, his face seemed expressionless, but there was something in his eye that made you feel that he thinks something is suspicious. "Let's warn Jess and Tess, before they eat any!" Frank whispered and they slowly tried to get the girls' attention and tell them.

"OH NO! Jess was realllllyyyy excited to eat these VANILLA-FLAVOURED Jammie Dodgers! WAAAA!" Jess cried, exaggerating.

"Tell the other guys about it!" Andrew whispered, "And tell them to pass it on!" he added.

"Okay!" said Tess, she didn't want anybody to die, so she was in a rush to tell them. They told Cara and Mia, who told Leo and Harry, who told Sinister. Smith who raised his eyebrows and told Chips. "Ridiculous! That makes no sense, though I do have to agree she did seem a bit suspicious - maybe we should not eat any!" Chips felt free to say, as the unusual lady had disappeared (or had she?). There was only five minutes left and they tried to enjoy them by eating their OWN non poisoned snacks. Though Frank said he couldn't because he had a tummy ache.

"Good thing I packed a packet of Vanilla-Flavoured Jammie Dodgers!" cheered Tess, looking inside her bag.

"YAYYYYYY!!!" Cried Jess in joy and happiness. "And I think I packed loads of white mice!" she added feeling excited for their mini feast. The coach was now approaching the tunnel and they were getting closer and closer to it. "I wonder what the tunnel is going to be like!" said Tess a bit loudly. Frank heard her and answered for her "It's going to be really **SCARY** and **MYSTERIOUS** with loads of $COBWEBS$ and it's going to be really **DARKKK** and – and -"

"ENOUGH FIBS! You know very well that The Tunnel will be NOTHING like that! No scariness, no mysteriousness, no cobwebs, it won't even be dark!" said Mia, irritated because he actually managed to scare the rest of them, especially Jess and Tess (no surprise there, because they're both scared of lots of things). They calmed down a bit, but they were about to find out that Mia was very wrong indeed ……

5
EYES IN THE BACK

The coach stopped right in front of the tunnel/cave entrance. It was very dark indeed, VERY DARK actually, even **darker** and **blacker** than Chips' shirt! It was very long too. The whole tunnel was 15 kilometres! And about twenty-five agencies were inside. Though very long, it was not very wide. It was only about 1.25 metres wide! So, if you were very fat – err - it may be a bit of a squeeze ….!

ANYWAY, the coach stopped outside and the Poor Bus Driver shouted, "ARRIVED!" to them. Mia took a deep breath, it indeed looked very scary and mysterious and cobwebby and dark! Meanwhile Frank was punching the air and shrieking "YESS!!" because the tunnel was exactly as he described. They started getting off, Andrew and Frank first, they all said 'Thank you' to the man and slowly went down the steps. The man was easily replying 'It's a pleasure!' and 'You're welcome!' but he stared at them in a way that he felt bad they had to go through this, and shook his head as they got off. Sinister. Smith just nodded at him and Chips acted as if they were best buddies. "Good Old Sam! Thanks for the trip, MATE! We'll send ya some richies when we win 'em!" she said as she put her arm round him.

"Um, thank you, now that'll be £9.78 …." Chips handed over the money with a very generous tip. "Thank you, Miss – Miss-?" he asked. Chips shook her head and slowly whispered something into his ear. He looked up and nodded to show he understood whatever Chips just told him. Half of the terrible group though that she said her UNKNOWN name, and the other half thought she told him that nobody knows her name and it was unknown. Well, whatever it was, they were all desperate to know, like you are! (I think?!) When they all got off, Sam Bus Driver gave them a beep and drove off, waving. As they were waving back, Cara saw something in the very back seat window that looked like a pair of eyes staring right at them! And on top of the eyes was a head with a red suit hat that only airplane people wear ……………

She gasped and shook Mia and whisper – shouted "THAT MYSTERIOUS NICE LADY WAS HIDING IN THE BACK SEATS!!!" her face looked pale and her eyes were wide open and twitching. "Chips! Chips! Chips! Chips!" they screamed and Chips looked at them and glared "What in the name of Richard Lewis do you want?!" she said, annoyed. They told her about what they had seen. The others listened and gasped. "Hmm …. I don't like the sound of some CHEEKY someone SPYING on us! I better call Sam." She took out her phone and called Sam's number, it took a long time but he eventually answered. "'Ello? Chips, is it? Want another ride 'ome or something?" he chuckled.

"VERY FUNNY Sam! But let me ask you a question, eh? Do you have some weird red airplane suited lady working on your bus? Does she serve drinks and snacks and stuff? Because there was a mysterious lady serving us some guessed **POISONED** snacks." explained Chips, also telling him that they saw her in the back. "'ed suited lady? 'n the back? Serving? 'ppeared ou' o' nowhere? No, I don't 'ave a serving 'ady on me 'us actually, 'et m' check the back now……" he said as his voice drifted away. There was a muffle and a bang, then the call suddenly ended ………..

The phone was just black darkness after that. *GULP* somebody gulped (most likely to be Jess). After a few seconds Chips broke the silence by saying, "Not to worry, Sam was probably just checking and his phone battery ran out …. not to worry…" she said as they stared into the darkness the coach disappeared in. They just stood there, holding their suitcases, jaws WIDEE open in shock, even Chips couldn't convince them …..

CLUP *CLUP* *CLUP* they heard footsteps behind them. It was a man coming out of the tunnel. He had a blue stripey shirt on and a red tie. He had a rope necklace thing around his neck that said in big letters,

DAVE MILLAR
STAFF: RED POTATOES; S.H.A

He saw them and said, "Aha! There you are! We have been waiting for you Red Potatoes! I am Dave, your Session Helper Assistant and Tour Guide! Let me lead you to your Safe Zone Bed...!" he seemed very jolly and nice, even if this wasn't going to be a NICE, jolly trip. They followed Dave, their S.H.A, into the darkness of all darknesses ....

6
DARKNESS

It was as, Frank said, **VERY, VERY** dark. It felt as if they were walking into the darkness of nothingness. Dave walked them past blood stains, pipes, **dead bodies**, weapons, steamy airs and loads of different rooms. After a long walk through the darkness, they arrived a room with a sign that said:

RED POTATOES SAFE ZONE BED
TWO BIG BEDS PROVIDED
ENJOY YOUR STAY!

Dave opened the door and they went through a small corridor and in front of them was two beds. But actually, TWO BEDS! I mean when they walked through the small corridor for five seconds in front of them was just two beds! No room to walk around or anything! Just two beds that fitted the small area perfectly. It was about 2.5 metres wide, and the beds took all the bed room space! "There's no room to move around in!!" complained Harry. Dave just smiled, "You won't be in your room most of the time! So why provide loads of space for no reason?" he answered. That made Harry shut up!

"But Harry is in his bed all day time! He doesn't even need lots of space!" Jess pointed out, giggling.

Harry went red and gritted his teeth at Jess, but Dave just laughed. "Get as much sleep as you want for the next two days, that's when the actual fighting begins! Feel free to unpack your things and relax!" he said, "I'll give you a tour tomorrow morning at 10am!" he adds before he walks out, leaving them in their <u>BED</u> room. "RIGHT!" said Chips, "ME and MR SMITH are going to have that beigey bed while YOU LOT share that creamy colour bed!" she commands. They all groan, they HATE sharing the same bed. "NO COMPLAINING!" she added, opening her suitcase and unpacking her stuff. Sinister Smith just took out a computer and started to type loads of things really quickly. "It's really dark in here, it feels like it's just **DARKNESS** all around us!" whispered Tess, feeling a bit scared. Everybody feels the same, they all feel scared from the $DARKNESS$. "It's okay Tessy! Let's share some snacks!" cheered Jess. They all search in their bags for sweets and they find precisely: 9 packets of Jammie Dodgers, 4 packets of bubblegum Squashies, 2 packs of salty popcorn, loads of Strawberry Dip Dabs, 3 packets of lemon sherbets, 17 packets of Skittles, 6 chocolate chip cookies, 41 packets of Walker's crisps, lots and lots of rainbow stripes and 91 fizzy sweets. "WOW I LOVE EATING SWEETS IN THE DARKNESS!!" cried Andrew happily.

"Tuck in!" Mia said, grabbing handfuls of fizzy sweets.

"**HOLD IT RIGHT THERE**!" shouted Chips. "YOU ARE NOT TO EAT ANY OF THOSE! YOU WILL GET REALLY **FAT** AND WILL BE

UNABLE TO WORK AND WALK PROPERLY! SO, YOU ARE ONLY ALLOWED MUESLI!!" she shrieked and folded her arms.

They all groaned miserably. Sweets were the best thing about it all! All This darkness didn't matter if they had sweets to eat. Though they *did* have sweets, but they WEREN'T allowed to eat any! Oh, man! Sad times.

"YOU ARE IN DISGRACE! YOU ALL ARE JUST TO SIT THERE DOING NOTHING, GROUNDED!" shouted Chips as she glared before going back to spiking her hair.

Chips has really spiky hair, and she often wore it in a very spiky ponytail.

"HUMPHH!" drooped Jess and sat down, head in her hands.

"This is like, soooooo boring!" said Frank and Leo sighed. So, they all just sat there in the darkness of darkness of all dark darkness rooms.

"This room couldn't have been darker!!" said Cara, unable to fall into her Cara Crab daydreams.

"I agree!" shivered Tess.

"AND we are not allowed to do anything!! Don't even ask me why Chips is being so strict!" shrugged Frank laughing a bit.

"No one actually WANTED to ask you Frank!!" Mia said sharply.

It made Andrew and Harry laugh.

"WHAT ARE YOU LAUGHING ABOUT!?" shouted Chips, glaring at them once more, "YOU'RE MEANT TO BE SITTING IN SILENCE, IN DISGRACE!!" Chips shouted even more.

"Sowwy Chips! It's just dat Mia and Fwank and Tess and Cara are being funny!!!" said Jess.

"STOP SPEAKING JESSICA! NO BODY ASKED YOUR OPINION! AND THE REST OF YOU BE QUIET!" Chips spat all over her face, because she was shouting so much. *Chips is so ridiculous!* Thought Mia *she's the one shrieking like a hooligan, just because we speak in the quietest voice!* Chips then goes back to spiking her hair. The dark room is once again very silent and even **DARKER**. Leo decided to sneaked some white mice from his bag and give them all one.

"Mmmmmm! Best thing about today!" said Jess, closing her eyes in delight.

"Makes this boring darkness room feel bright!" whispered Frank savouring every mouthful.

So, they just sat there pretending to eat the muesli while actually sneaking sweets. Sinister. Smith was still on his computer. But he excitedly and randomly shouted, "LOOK! I MANAGED TO HACK THROUGH THE COMPUTER SYSTEM! AND NOW I CAN SEE WHERE EVERYONE IS! SO, IF ONE OF YOU DIE, IT'LL APPEAR ON THE SCREEN!" he shouted, jumping up and down with the computer in his hands. "Lemme see that then!" said Chips. He handed the computer over and Chips looks at the screen and looks impressed. "Good job! Old Steven Smith has done something GREAT!" she said, "You kids should LEARN from this genius!" Sinister. Smith was glad Chips appreciated what he did. Like, just IMAGINE Chips calling you a genius! The children, all had different thoughts, here are a few: *can we get some more sleep to celebrate Sinister. Smith's genius?* **Harry wondered.** *Wow, so you can impress Chips, by just doing a few tricks on a computer?* **Cara thought.** *Why is that so genius?! Does Chips physically WANT a thing that tells her we're dead!?* **Thought Leo.** *HUMPH! Why can't I do something amazing to make Chipsy Chispy call me a genius?!* **Mia was thinking.** *'Cause you're not a genius DUH!* **Frank added into her thoughts.** *SHUT UP!* **Came her mind reply.** Sinister. Smith had gone back to his computer, trying to make something more impressive, so Chips may even give him a gold star! He smiled in his mind at the thought.

Hours went by and The Terrible Group felt more bored than ever. It was until Dave came back up; they perked up a bit.

"I will be showing you around today and telling you the rules of how to play!" he said, in his great jolly voice.

"But you said you were coming tomorrow, not today!" exclaimed Harry, he actually wanted to stay in bed, not walk around a tunnel learning how to play a 'game' he already knew how to play. "Change of schedule! Today's the tour tomorrow's the hunt!" Dave told him, with a big beamy smile.

"Do we get food?" Asked an eager Tess, she wanted to eat really badly because she was absolutely STARVING. "Yes, I think your S.H.M would be willing to feed you!" answered Dave. He knew the answer to almost EVERYTHING.

"Our S.H.M? What's that?" asked Mia, all these S.Hs we're confusing her.

"Session Helper Manager, I'm just an assistant, he's the real boss, our Jack," he answered once more.

"Is that his name? Jack?" asked Andrew.

"Yes, blow me, that's his name! Now enough questions and let's get crackin'!" he led them through the corridor and out the door. It was still really dark outside. "Is it going to be dis dark when we go out tomorrow?" Jess wanted to know.

"Hmmm ... actually no, I don't think so! There will be candles placed this evening for tomorrow!"

"As you can see, there are many different rooms, this whole tunnel area is just safe zones," he said as they passed many doors with different signs, like:

TOILET NAILS SAFE ZONE BED
FOUR SMALL BEDS PROVIDED
EMJOY YOUR STAY!

and

THE GLOBS SAFE ZONE BED
ONE BUNK BED PROVIDED
ENJOY YOUR STAY!

and

CHOCOLATE WORLD SAFE ZONE BED
SIX MINI BEDS PROVIDED
ENJOY YOUR STAY!

"Chocolate World are our friends," Jess told Dave, but he just shook his head. "Nobody's your friend here lass, you're all fighting for the riches!" he said, which made Jess feel sad, because Chocolate World were always nice to them. "There are lots of workers here, that work in the mining areas, so please don't mistaken them for enemies and kill them!

"There are no bathrooms, so you will have to pee when no one's looking or behind a cardboard box or something,"

"There is a killing kitchen here that you can make poisonous foods and trick people! There are some really dark rooms, that only pros can enter, it is really dark and impossible to see your enemy!" *But it's impossible to see here! No difference then!* Thought Cara. "I will show you that in a minute. Now as the tunnel is 15 km long, it fits lots of people, so you will see people EVERYWHERE, you need to be careful and every time you see someone, threaten them or ask questions, you seem good at that! Find out more and kill them if really necessary. Some people here actually don't work for anybody, so you can try and convince them to join your team, by giving them a good amount of salary and competitive tasks, then jolly well good, you've got yourself a new member!"

They approached a door that had a sign which said:

DO NOT ENTER (BUT I KNOW YOU'RE GOING TO ENTER ANYWAY, BUT I JUST PUT THE SIGN UP FOR THE CASH)

Please give the cash to Simone Katherine Elliot. (the writer)

"That's our Simone. She puts up the signs and sometimes adds a few bits to them, as you can see!" He opened the door. "This is the Pro Room I was talking about!" And indeed, he opened a door to a room that was definitely a dark darkness room. "Are we going in?" gulped Jess.

"No lassie, it's way too scary for you now, we may see in a couple of weeks or so!" said Dave, making them breathe with relief.

"That's a shame!" said Harry, "I wanted to go in there!" and Dave laughed, "Another day lad, just not today, I'll tell you that for sure!" and Harry sighed.

7
WONDER

(NOTE: This is a small chapter but has a few things to think about)

"There's just a few more places I have to show you before I send you back," said Dave as he closed The Pro Room door and led them in a different direction. "We have a meeting with Jack in about ten minutes in the Killing Kitchen," he said, looking at his watch. "So, before then I shall take you to the Historical Room to learn a few facts about yourselves!" he added, opening a small door with a sign that said:

HISTORICAL ROOM (THE HSITORY OF YOUR LIFE, LAYS IN THIS VERY ROOM)

From the very scientific words by Simone Katherine Elliot.

"Simone wrote that too, right?" asked Tess, looking at the extra bit.

"How did you guess?" replied Dave with a smile, as he held the door open for them to get in. "It says it right there!!" answered Jess for her, as she pointed to Simone's name and looked at the paintings and pictures on the walls. They passed many doors with different signs. "Apple Pies, Bubble Boys, The Globs, Red Poetoes ……" He stopped for a second, then turned to the right. "Aha! Red Potatoes!" true enough, right in front of them was a door that said;

RED POTATOES HISTORY (EVERYTHING YOU NEVER KNEW ABOUT YOURSELF)

Written and manufactured by Simone Katherine Elliot.

"Simone deffo sounds like a joker," said Frank as he read the sign. "You could say that about yourself, Frank!" replied Cara. "I quite like the messages, though, they're pretty funny!" she added. Dave smiled, "She'd appreciate that lass, she loves being called funny! Now then my friends, let's find out more!" he said, in that jolly voice of his. They saw pictures of people that looked French *Perhaps they're our ancestors!* Cara thought.

Chips suddenly stopped and pointed at a picture, "Look here children! This is our first ancestor! Jackson Bridge! He is the founder of The Red Potatoes!" she told them, and they all looked eagerly at this mysterious ancestor of theirs. "Indeed, you are right Chips, this is the founder of Red Potatoes! He may not be your REAL ancestor, as you're not related to Chips, but he is the founder of your agency!" Dave said as Chips beamed with pride. "Now let's move on to the library section, we just have a bit of time to look before the meeting!" he said, leading them to an area with a small sign that said;

LIBRARY (RED POTATOES LIBRARY, NOT ANY OTHER SILLY AGENCY)

Said sharply by the brilliant Simone Katherine Elliot

"History ... Generations ... Fights ...." Dave muttered as he looked at the spine of books. "........... Children! There it is! 'The Amazing Children of The Red Potatoes! Now children let me just see the years......." He flicked through loads of pages; they saw the words 'Chips' and 'Red Poetoes' and 'Enemies' and 'Cookies and Cream' multiple times. "........... Early 2000s! Perfect! Now should we skip the intro?" he asked, looking up at them.

"No, I'm sure they'd want to hear a bit of intro," Chips said, and they nodded.

"Righty-Hoo! Does anyone know why they actually work here? Or HOW they ended up here? Well, this very book holds the answers! So you will find out!" he whispered dramatically, "So now- OH WAIT I'm so sorry but the meeting is in two minutes!" Dave said frantically as he shut the book and put it back on the shelf. "We can't be late! We have to move you know!" he said, as they quickly made their way out of the library and ran over to the Killing Kitchen. The whole trip to the History place thing got everyone thinking deeply. *How DID we get here?* They all thought *how did we end up working here?* They wondered I hope you are wondering too, the trip may not have gave them, or you information, but it gave you something to think about and wonder. How DID they start working there? You may soon find out ……. (later)

8
JACK SPURS

"Hurry up Potatoes! Jack is expecting us!" Dave said as they ran over to the kitchen with the very comical sign:

THE KILLING KITCHEN (ALSO KNOWN AS THE KITCHEN OF DOOM THAT YOU <u>WON'T</u> SURVIVE!)

Written and created by the Oh So Smart, Simone Katherine Elliot.

He opened the door and there was a young-looking man probably the age of twenty or so, leaning on the wall. There were two bodyguards with weapons on either side of him. He had slick blonde hair, green eyes and wore quite shabby clothes; old shirt and trousers.

"Ah, there you are! What took you so long, eh?" he smiled as he shook hands with Dave. "Fussy man you are Jack! Do you call thirty seven seconds late, late?" he grinned, as Jack patted his back. Jack smiled over at the children and said, "Aha! So, you must be my pretty little agents! You look like a tough lot! I think this will work out pretty well!" he said cheerfully, looking at them. "I am Jack Spurs, your Session Helper Manager! I will be leading you all, to the riches! Now kids, I want you all to say your full names and something about yourselves," he said. He pointed at Frank. "You first, then the person beside you, then beside you, and so on..." he said, nodding at every person. "Ok then! I'm Frank Alex Bill Johnson and I'm a tough-nut that puts people in their place!" he swaggered, showing off the muscles he didn't have. Jack nodded and pointed his pen at Andrew.

"I'm Andrew Smith and I like reading SPY books, and spying on people!" he said.

"I am Leo Brooks and I like killing and missions AND stealing biscuits!" laughed Leo, slicking his hair backwards.

"I'm Harry Petersss and I LOVE sleep and killer socks!" Harry said, a bit lazily.

"**I'm Mia Ruth Badger, and I have a very loud voice and a great talent of killing and spying**," said Mia, confidently stepping forwards.

"I AM Jessica Lucy Badger, or just call me Jess, and I am good at....ummm... eating Jammie Dodgers and being annoying!" said Jess, giggling.

"I am Tess Garcia and I am very kind and love doing missions," said Tess sweetly, with a big smile.

"I'm Cara Michaels and I LOVE crabs and going on missions, oh, and being the boss!" said Cara, laughing. Jack nodded slowly.

"Great! We have a different selection of people here, I'm sure we can make this work. Anyway, I better introduce myself a bit more too!" he gave a great big beamy smile. "I'm Jack Spurs and I am a big Spurs supporter......."

"UMMM? NO, YOU'RE NOT! LIVERPOOL FOR LIFE!!" Frank shouted.

"NO WAY, COME ON UNITED!" Shrieked Leo punching the air.

"ITS ACTUALLY ARSENAL YOU IDIOTS!!" yelled Cara.

"NAHH! IT HAS TO BE MAN UNITED! SUIIIIII!" screamed Harry.

"YEAH! SUUIIIIIIEEEEE!" screeched Tess. She was so loud they nearly deafened!

"NOT A CHANCE! ITS LIVERPOOL YOU DUMMIES!" shrieked Mia.

"YEAH, ITS DEFFO LIVERPOOL!" screamed Andrew.

"Errr – umm - Southampton?" said Jess, hopefully. Everyone stopped.

"NAH! That's WAYYY off the scale Jess," said Mia.

"Pathetic!" agreed Cara, nodding.

"Absolutely ridiculous!" said someone.

"Has she lost her mind?" said another.

"WAIT! Jess, Liverpool or Man U?" said Frank.

"Errrrrc – ummmm - Man U?"

"YESSS!" screamed Leo and Harry, jumping on her shoulders.

"LIVERPOOL!"

"MAN UNITED!"

"MAN UNITED!"

"ARSENAL!"

"LIVERPOOL!"

"ARSENAL!" even Chips was joining in!

"MAN U! SUIII!"

"NO! LIVERPOOL!"

"SOUTH HAMPTON!!!!"

Jack smiled at this determined, but loud agency and then said,

"Alright then, calm down now……" they settled. "I know you all have different opinions, but Spurs is definitely the best-"

"HEY, HEY, HEY! WE ALREADY DISCUSSED THIS!"

"LIVERPOOOOOOOL IS THE BEST!"

"NO ARSENAL IS!!!"

Jack was now laughing and trying to settle them down.

"ALRIGHT! That's enough now," he said as they all fell silent.

"Now, as I was saying- I am Jack Spurs, your S.H.M, and I am a

MASSIVE Spurs supporter, as my name says! I am twenty-five years old and will be helping you win the riches! But I do expect A BIT of the riches if you win, because I would've helped you win!" Then, he laughed.

"A few diamonds would be good!!" added Dave, sputtering.

"AND a ruby or two!" Jack added and then the two men starting laughing so much they clutched their tummies and their faces went red. "HEY! HOLD IT RIGHT THERE!! What if you do a BAD job and den we lose?" glared Jess, folding her arms. They fell quiet immediately.

"Good point," muttered Dave, and Jack nudged him in a *be-quiet!* sort of way.

"Anyway guys," started Jack, completely ignoring Jess's question.

"Here I will be giving advice and telling you how to win and kill and stuff, with Dave assisting me." And Dave nodded. Then took out a map of the tunnel and a few guns. He started giving examples, pointing to directions on the map, telling them HOW to kill, what method, what weapons, what emotion to show. They spent two hours doing that, before they called it a night and went back to their safe zone bed. As they got into their pyjamas and snuggled to bed, Chips said, "RIGHT THEN! Tomorrow's the big day! I want you to put ALL effort into this! And whatever you do, DON'T. YOU. DARE. DIE!"

They nodded and said, 'Okay Chips!' and 'Will do!' and 'Yes Miss!', But they were ALL secretly scared. What did she mean don't die? Of course, they didn't WANT to die! But did Chips actually care THIS much, she didn't want them to die? Frank smirked and went to bed, like the rest of them had.

9
GETTING READY

It was exactly six o'clock when two guards, dressed in military gear, came knocking at their door. In fact, they didn't even knock, they just barged straight in and woke The Red Potatoes up.

"Wake up and get ready to get going," said one of them, who had darker skin and a wrist watch.

"Yes, Sir Jack told us to wake you up, so you can be ready earlier," said the other. He had quite pale skin and dirty blonde hair, while the other was completely bald.

The Red Potatoes immediately got dressed in matching 'Red Potatoes' shirts. It wasn't their usual one, this type was black and dark so they didn't stand out.

"Now," started the bald one, "Jack said he wanted Frank, Leo, Mia, Andrew and Cara to go off first. Then, when they come back for a break, someone else goes instead. And keep rotating so everybody gets out," he said

"And he also said that you could go in pairs if you like," added blonde-haired dude.

"Oh, AND keep looking for clues, like letters, numbers, notes or trails could ALL come in useful," said bald one as they went out.

They sat in silence for a few minutes before Andrew asked, "Chips, will you and Sinister. Smith go out too?" Sinister. Smith looked up at the mention of his name.

"Firstly, his name is MR SMITH, you are expected to call him that. SECONDLY, have you lost your mind? WHY would we be here if we literally aren't going to do anything?" she answered, glaring at him.

"Soooooooooo, is that a, yes?" he asked, innocently.

"YES! OF COURSE WE ARE! ARE YOU PURPOSELY BEING DUMB??!!?" she shouted. Not a pretty face, huh.

There was another few minutes of silence before Chips looked at her watch and said, "Just another two minutes now, you should really....."

"YOU SHOULD REALLY START GETTING READY!" said Dave in a jolly voice as if they were not just about to go out and possibly get killed.

"AHEM. Excuse me Mr. David, I do not like being interrupted, okay? Now, do we need to go out now, or in a few minutes?"

"FIRSTLY, my name is DAVE, only my mother calls me David. SECONDLY, yes, you have to go out now, ARE YOU PURPOSELY BEING DUMB??!!?" he said, while winking at the children.

Chips went red with embarrassment and glared at Dave, while the children stared at him in awe.

RINGGGG - RINGGG - RINGGGGGG

"That's the bell, it means you have to go now," he said. "Wishing you all the best of luck!" he added.

"Mia, Frank, Leo, Cara and Andrew, please step forward," said Chips. And they did.

"Show me your guns, knives and TNTs," she ordered. And they did so.

"Now, off you go!" she commanded, firmly.

10
INTO THE TUNNEL OF MURDER

Mia went off quickly (but a bit timidly) with a serious face. She wanted to look like she meant business, but in reality, she didn't.

She slowly looked around, and, like Dave said, there was some lit candles so you could see a bit better. She had a feeling some candles had already been used for killing.

On the other hand, Frank was striding confidently and looked around every now and then to make sure he wasn't being followed.

He picked one of the candles and used it as a torch, *It may come in handy!* He thought.

Cara was loitering in a corner at first, because she felt she needed a moment to take this all in. So, she tried to calm herself down. *Now then, Cara Crab.* She thought. *You need to calmmmmmm ittt downnnn! I know your scared because you've just went out into the tunnel of murder, but relax, it's not like your gonna die! Are you a woman or − err - a mouse?* Then Cara FINALLY decided to calm down and go out and investigate and look for clues and kills.

"Here we go into the tunnel of murder! Do Laa Laa! Do Laa Laa! I hope I won't die, *Dooo Laaaaa*

$\mathcal{L}aaaaa$!" she sang (she is really bad at singing, if you were there your ears would have fallen off!)

She met a couple of people on the way, which was surprising, as it was only early and not many people would be out. She knocked out three and chatted to four.

Of course, Cara checked behind her, every minute or two, to make sure she wasn't being followed, twice she seen someone and knocked them out, but a few times, when she looked back it felt as if someone was behind her, but she couldn't see anybody.

MYSTERIOUS.

Poor Leo was having a hard time. As soon as he went out, he bumped into someone. When I mean 'bumped' I mean really bumped! He wasn't looking where he was going, and full on **BUMPED** into somebody. This somebody immediately turned around and pointed the gun at Leo.

"PUT YOUR HANDS RIGHT WHERE I CAN SEE THEM OR I'LL PUT A BULLET THROUGH YOUR HEAD!" yelled the person.

"YES SIR!" said Leo immediately. He put his gun down and slowly put his hands up.

"Who are you and who do you work for?" the man asked.

"I'm - err - Sam Thinghead and I work for – err - Things!" he replied with a nervous laugh.

"Yeah right, what do you think I am? An idiot?"

"No, I think you're an absolute dumbhead who I will knock out in five seconds," said Leo, and as he finished his sentence he jumped onto the man, and using his super karate skills, he kicked the man right on the chin knocking him out.

"Well, that was easy," he muttered to himself as he dusted his hands. Little did he know, back-up we're coming.

About ten or eleven men came running holding guns and shouting at Leo to put his ping-stick arms in the air.

Poor Leo used up ALL his karate, kung-fu, ju-jitsu, judo and material art skills on them. And while doing that, he ended up with multiple bruises on his face, loads of scars on his arms and a few cuts on his hands and knees. BUT he did knock them all out, so that was a goal achieved.

"Well, that was VERY easy," he muttered to himself sarcastically, as he dusted his swollen hands.

While that was happening, Andrew was having troubles FINDING anybody!

He walked cautiously, holding the gun tightly while looking for clues and people to question or knock out.

He heard voices and gunshots near the Killing Kitchen, so headed over there. First, he looked at the sign, pardon me, first he looked at where the sign was MEANT to be. Poor Simone, her signs had been ripped off completely, leaving little shreds of paper around.

He was about to go in, until something caught his eye, on one of the tiny pieces of paper there was a letter that was written in big capitals in deep black. It looked different to the other letters He looked closely at the paper and saw it said;

T

He gasped, this was a clue! He ran and ran and ran back to the safe zone and arrived out of breath. Luckily Chips, Jess, Tess
and Harry were still there.

"CHIPS, CHIPS, CHIPS, CHIPS, CHIPS, CHIPS!" he screamed.

"Whatever is the matter screaming-boy? I was just about to go out until you came in screaming like a hooligan!"

"No need to be spiteful! Guess what I've found! A CLUE!" he said, shoving the note in her face.

It took Chips a moment to take it all in. And then she suddenly screamed,

"HOORAY!"

They had only been there for five minutes, and they had already found a clue?! Chips was so happy she was on cloud nine for the rest of the day. The thought of their chances of winning getting higher, made Chips feel EXCITED inside. She congratulated Andrew and two minutes later, came a very tired and bruised looking Leo.

"I NEED A BREAK PLEASE! I HAVE JUST BEEN SEVERELY ATTACKED BY A BUNCH OF GLOBS!!" he shouted before collapsing on the floor.

"Oh dear, somebody's had a day, before the day even started! Tess and Harry, you can go out now, Jessica, you stay here with Leo and go out when you can, OH and tell the others about the clue IF they come" she said before leaving the room. That 'IF they come' worried them.

Tess wondered off, determined to be useful in some way, she got her gun ready and went out in ACTION!

"What HAPPENED to you?" asked Jess, looking at his injuries with a concerned look on her face.

"Got in a bit of trouble, you know," he answered. Jess didn't know, she didn't get a chance to go out. And the feeling of missing out made Jess physically ACHE to go out.

"I think I should go now, tell anybody about the clue WHEN they come," said Jess, purposely saying WHEN and not IF so not to scare them.

After she left Leo thought to himself, *gosh, I've never heard Jess sound so serious and not babyish!* Before closing his eyes and trying to get some rest.

***

While they were out, the rest of the agency were PARTYING their secret 'Simon the Snake' socks off. Miss Mush made them her very RARE and DELICIOUS cookies and cream (the agency are literally IN LOVE with cookies and cream. And will go mad if they see any) and chocolate chip-cookies and red velvet *cupcakes* and chest nut cream meringues and hot chocolates with peaks of cream and walnut cakes and fairy cakes and doughnuts and éclairs ANDDDDDD my mouth is watering just thinking of it. I'm sure yours is too, so I better shut up about the food.

They were wearing comfortable and disco clothes instead of their 'Red Potatoes' matching shirts. They had pillows and party games and food (of course, how could we forget ?!) and a live concert playing and farm yard animals all around the place and an alien visitor and a unicorn giving out slime and anything else you can possibly imagine !

EVERYBODY was partying, even the 'Good Group' ! There was Miss Mush and Alex Basil and Love Texas and Tom Millar and Vicky and Hannah Walters and Florence First Aid and Sarah Lincoln and Ellie Group and Elena Williams and a whole lot of other agents and yes I know you don't know half of the people there but, oh well.

In case you haven't guessed yet, they were partying because Chips was gone as well as the 'Terrible Group', but mainly Chips anyway. They found this an opportunity for a BREAK from spying, killing and missions, so they decided to make the most of it. I'm sure you would have too. Because believe me, Chips never allowed any one to have fun or enjoy anything.

Chips' motto was; *your life doesn't belong to you, so you can't have fun with it.* Don't even question the life bit. Chips believes that your life belongs to your parents or saviours, because you wouldn't be alive if it wasn't for them.

So while The Terrible Group and Chips and Mr. Smith were risking their lives (that apparently don't belong to them) the rest of the agency were having the best time of THEIR lives (that apparently don't belong to them) partying and *enjoying* their free time.

If Chips' motto was to not have fun, Jess's motto was *life is like a big rollercoaster. You can either enjoy your moment or scream at the top of your lungs. If I were you, I'd enjoy the moment. BECAUSE LIFE IS ABOUT FUNNNNN.* Sounds very professional, until you get to the last bits. Like, please be realistic, this is Jess we are talking about, of course she has to be a bit silly!

11
FINDING CLUES

If I go on telling you exactly what everyone done, this book would be a thousand pages long. So, I will just tell you the inner details you'd even WANT to know. Like clues or interesting moments they had, because I don't think you want to know about every step they had or every breath they took. So yeah, back to the point.

Tess went down with a glare in her eyes. Her whole body was shaking, but she tried to ignore that feeling. She wanted to do some- thing impressive. She wanted to do something amazing. Something mind-blowing, something spectacular, something so great that nobody would EVER tease her again.

And she knew just where to go. She headed straight to The History Room. She had a feeling that it was a perfect place for a clue or a trail or even a knock out. *Because if I was a Richard Lewis, I'd hide clues in a place hardly anybody would go. Because they are here for riches not a history lesson.* She thought as she headed down the corridor. Then, she heard footsteps,

CLOMP, CLOMP, CLOMP

they went. So, she immediately tuned around quickly. It was a man, who looked in his late thirties. He was wearing big brown boots with baggy trousers that grandpas wear and a blue blazer with The Takeaway Timers logo on it.

He looked surprised to see Tess there but got his sense back and aimed his gun at her.

"STAY RIGHT THERE!" he shouted while Tess did as she was told and stayed still.

"Who are you then, kid?" he asked, peering at her.

"An agent," she replied boldly.

"A little lass like you? You must be eight if not younger! Stop mucking about kid, you must be a staff's daughter or a trespasser. Because nobody would want a skinny little thing like you in their agency,"

"I'll thank you not to insult me," she said with an edge to her voice. She clenched her fists.

"You funny-little sausage, thinking you can get the better of me. Do you even know who I am? Carlos Walters, you probably have never even heard of me!" he laughed. "Though, DO you know who I am?"

Tess did know who he was, Carlos Walters, multi-billionaire spy working for The Takeaway Timers. No, that was a lie, he was PRETENDING to work for them, he actually works for The Globs. One of the best agencies in the world.

"You with me here kid? Or are you on your own planet? Planet Nutty perhaps," he laughed. His voice sounded really high-pitched.

Enough was enough, Tess rugby-tackled him to the ground and using her new kung-fu skills, knocked him out.

"Now that's what I call funny!" said Tess before noticing that a piece of paper had fell out of his pocket. It said this;

My spine is stiff, my body is pale, I'm always ready to tell a tale. What am I?

Tess knew exactly what this was. A riddle that would lead to a clue. She just needed the answer.

Think Tess, she thought.

Think

Think

Think

Think

Think

Think

thinkkkkkkkkkkkkkkk . . . . . .

AHA! Tess got it! It was so obvious! A BOOK!! What other thing had a stiff spine and was always ready to tell a tale? Wait ….. where could you find books? A Library of course! And Tess was heading the right direction. Maybe Carlos was trying to go to the Library too.

***

Harry was in the middle of the tunnel somewhere. He felt lazy but started waking up as he went. He had already questioned and knocked out seventeen. BUT he hadn't found a single clue. Not a sausage. Not a crumb. He began fiddling with his gun carelessly and accidently shot the air. He had attracted four or five German Nightmares, who were coming at him with machine guns. Rumour said that the German Nightmares were REALLY good at figuring out riddles and clues and always had their eyes open and never missed a thing. That could have been true because Harry saw their pockets positively **STUFFED** with paper pieces.

Harry immediately pointed his gun and turned around to look at every single one of them. They simply smiled.

"Er ist nur ein kind, lasst uns nur geben ihn eins von unser besonderen stattdessen!" said the biggest one. He was obviously the leader of the group. And they were all obviously The German Nightmares, because they had just spoken in German. They obviously thought Harry couldn't speak German. But he understood every single word, in translation they said;

'He is just a kid, let's just give him one of our special ones instead,'

A thin one with glasses and black curly hair took out a piece of paper that had a riddle on it. He gave it to Harry and they walked off. The riddle was;

I have hands but no arms, a face but no eyes. What am I?

Harry was stunned. Did they just give him a riddle that would lead to a clue? Weren't they against him? Something was fishy, did they already use the riddle and got the clue? Or had they just been trying to be nice?

'He is just a kid, let's just give him one of our special ones instead'

Those were the man's words. Maybe he meant special gifts? Or special surprises, because the surprise was that they give him a clue? Harry looked very young for his age, so maybe they just wanted to be nice to him? Thought he was a little kid and decided to give him a favour? Harry decided to go back to the safe zone and tell whoever was there, what had happened to him.

He arrived and saw Sinister Smith and Mia looking at Sinister Smith's computer. Sinister. Smith was typing something and Mia was peering over his shoulder. He stamped his feet and they both looked up, a bit surprised to see him and then Mia said, "Yes? Anything the matter then?" in a stern kind of voice.

"Well yes actually, there were these German Nightmare dudes, and they said in German, 'He's just a kid, let's give him one of our special ones,' and then this dude took out a riddle-clue and gave it to me and they walked off, so as much as I'd love a free clue, it's kind of suspicious that they'd just give me one and we are enemies," he explained.

Mia and Sinister. Smith looked at each other for a second before, Sinister. Smith looked at Harry and cleared his voice before saying, "Hmmm, interesting, very interesting. Bring it here then boy, I need to examine it," he said in his flattest voice. He always wanted to look and speak dull and boring and flat because he didn't want to show his feelings or emotions or give anything away. He actually tried to avoid talking most the time.

Harry walked over to them and showed them the note he was given. There was a ruby on Sinister. Smith's lap. After he gave the note, he looked at the ruby and asked Mia, "What's that?" pointing to it.

"Oh, Sinister. Smith found it on the floor and he thought it may have fell out of the bag when Richard Lewis was hiding the riches. He's also examining it and checking for finger prints and DNA and all that stuff. I was already here, taking a break when Sinister. Smith came, so I just stayed with him," she replied.

"That's Mr. Smith to you!" he muttered gruffly, before saying, "This is the note Garcia found," Sinister. Smith has a habit of calling people by their surname. "As you can see, both notes have curly, fancy writing and a riddle. But I have examined more clearly, and seen that the handwriting is slightly different AND when I looked even deeper, I seen that the pieces of paper is different. The one that Garcia found is sort of cream, like ivory, made and manufactured by Lewis Crafts. But this one is different. It's pure white. Ugly white, and it's manufactured by Winston & Co. So, I hate to say Peters, but this one given too you," he said lifting it up, "Is a fake!" he said dramatically, showing the tiniest bit of emotion.

"These Germanos are probably giving out fake riddles and clues to stop people from winning the riches! You can't trust anybody here Harry, and when they said they'll give you one of their special ones instead, they probably meant they'd give you a 'clue' instead of a knock out or even a kill!" said Mia.

"Good point! Where is Chips now?" asked Harry curiously.

"Chips? She went with Tess to the library to see if they could find a clue, and guess what?? Jack thought of an amazing plan, that could help us win the riches! Want me to tell you??"

After Mia and Sinister. Smith told Harry the amazing plan Jack had thought of, and he agreed it was a good plan they went out again. Little did they know that a very mysterious someone had heard the whole conversation and now knew what The Red Potatoes were up too .....

12
LILA HART

Mia quickly got out of the Safe Zone and went out into the darkness. She was determined to NOT make the same mistake as Harry. Even though it wasn't completely a mistake, he was still dumb enough to believe it was real, even if just for a second.

Mia desperately wanted to do something good. Even TESS had been super useful. She wanted to find a clue or a riddle or a note of some kind. She looked and looked and looked and even started getting a bit careless. But she knew she had to be careful. Because if you get careless or mad about something, you could easily make really dumb mistakes. And gosh, would that be embarrassing.

She seen a few people in the way. They were mostly coward agencies. Like Creepy Crawlies and Aliens 'n' America and Marvel Kids and Wannabe Bears and so on and so on.

After many, many cowardy agencies, Mia thought maybe that this area of the tunnel was probably where all the 'wannabe' and 'uncool' and (of course) 'cowardy' agencies were. So, she decided to go deeper into the tunnel where most of the 'better' agencies were.

She was walking very, very slowly because, there was a heck lot of people in that area and she had already bumped into nine and knocked all of them out.

Voices, gunshots, screaming, footsteps. That was all Mia could hear. She could hardly even hear her heart beats or the breaths she was taking. *Maybe I've gone in a bit TOO deep!* She thought to herself as she decided to go the other way. She turned around and saw a girl standing, staring at her.

She stood up and aimed the gun at the girl and examined her properly. She had long dramatic blonde hair, angel blue eyes, flawless teeth, long nails and she looked about Mia's age. She was one of those girls who could act perfect, who enjoyed getting other girls she was jealous of into trouble. If you ever seen her in a shop, she'd be walking perfectly with a shopping cart that would also, be walking perfectly, because she was one of those girls, that even their shopping carts are always as perfect as them. (not like one of those wonky carts that are hard to move with).

She stared at Mia with a little smirk on her face. It was obvious she was waiting for Mia to say something first.

"Stay right there or I'll put a bullet through your face!" Mia commanded.

The girl smirked some more. She was holding a silver M191 but she wasn't using it. She didn't even aim.

"Who are you and who do you work for?" Mia asked, quite loudly.

The girl fluttered her big eyelashes and just stared at Mia.

"I SAID WHO ARE YOU AND WHO DO YOU WORK FOR??"

The girl just stared at her with a satisfied grin on her face. She was clearly enjoying annoying Mia.

"If you don't speak up, I'll rip that pinky-winky smile off your face with a bullet. SO. SPEAK. UP!" Mia was started to lose her patience.

The girl's smirk, changed into a scowl, she glared at Mia before saying, "Um, no need to lose your temper or anything like, my name's Lila Hart and I work for the Red Poetoes, so like, what's it to you?" she said with this false, dinky American accent.

"Lila Hart, eh? Sounds familiar ….." said Mia with a grin as memories started flooding back to her.

Lila immediately recognized Mia. "Ugh, it's you little imperfect, pesky Badger girl, you stole our Belle and ruined everything!"

Which was true, Mia had leered Isabelle Clanks, over to Red Potatoes. And to this day, Isabelle works for The Red Potatoes.

"So then Little Miss Perfect, what are you going to do about it? Go cry to your precious little leader-weader daddy-waddy?" Mia said. It was because Lila's father, Mac Hart, is the leader of The Red Poetoes.

Lila's face went red, "You shut up you pathetic little nobody. You think you're so cool and brave but your just another little pesky-weirdo girls who are just worthless insects," said Lila, making her blue-angel eyes go big and twitchy.

"And you're just a little jealous cow, thinking you are so perfect but you're a little brat who can't say boo to a goose! And you stop making them stupid girlie eye glares with me, you-wee piece of filth!"

"There she goes again, insulting everyone, that's probably your hobby. But believe me, Mia you CANNOT get the better of me. I'm Lila Hart, the perfectest-bestest-bravest-sweetest-friendliest-coolest-strongest-girl in the world. Everybody loves me!" she said, flicking her hair.

"If you're so strong and brave and cool, how about you prove that to me in a karate match, what do you say wee-baby-Lily?" Mia said with a smirky-grin and glary eyes.

"Lila! KARATE? Is that the best you've got?" she said, flicking her hair again in the most annoying manner, "I know karate, judo, ju-jitsu and kung-fu!! See? So now I'm probably the most extraordinary person you'll ever meet, rat!"

"Ooh how lovely! The stupid little girlie brat knows another move or two. So what? I know judo, ju-jitsu, kung-fu, material arts, martial arts, thai arts AND karate, so don't worry girlie, you're miles behind!"

"You may know a BIT more skills than me, but that doesn't make you any better, you're a devil, you TORTURED my best friend, Ariana, and then threw her in the sea! You killed her! You're a monster!"

Ariana Porter, aged twenty. She was sent on a mission to kill Chips AND Mia. Red Poetoes and Red Potatoes were at the biggest war ever at the time, and Mia had become really useful, so Ariana had to kill both Chips and Mia. While she was on the mission,

Chips found out that Ariana had been spying on them for weeks and weeks and she was the one who destroyed the ship they were planning to use as a secret weapon. There was fifteen people on the ship. They all died. Red Potatoes have sworn revenge on Ariana, and when Mia caught her on Ariana's mission to kill them, that's what they did. Revenge.

"Meh, meh, meh like a goat. That's exactly what you are Lila, a stupid little goat. And that Ariana business isn't my fault, Ariana got what she deserves the little cow, and *I* didn't kill her. She died because she can't swim. Which is her own fault, the stroppy little brat!"

"Shut up Mia! You're nothing but a stupid, ugly, heartless monster who killed my friend and STOLE my friend and made my life misery! But since I'm the extraordinary girl I am, I stayed patient and unlike you, fat ugly piglet, I'm a calm, patient person!" said Lila and started crying.

"Keep the insults to kids your size, and you are not going to fool me, I'm not falling for that baby-crying joke. You're just a baby who's trying to get me to feel concern for you. Don't worry, I'm not fallin' for it!" said Mia.

Lila got so mad she lunged towards Mia. Luckily, Mia dodged and Lila went flying to the floor, face-first.

"Whoopsie! Temper, temper! Has the little cry-baby, lost her wee-temper?"

"Shut up you insulting-piece of filth!"

"Hah! Prove you're so cool and amazing in a fight! Kung-fu, karate, ju-jitsu, material arts, anything you like!"

"Deal on Badger!"

"BUT, firstly, do you have any clues or riddles, Little Lila?" Mia asked curiously.

"Loads!" replied Lila taking out three notes.

"Same here, so the loser has to give the winner their clues!"

"You Badgers have always been so greedy! Fine, deal on!"

"Right then, Hart, let's go find ourselves an area to fight in,"

Actually, Mia didn't have any clues or riddles or evidence or anything. She was very pleased she managed to fool Lila.

They found themselves a big area to fight in (The Killing Kitchen, actually,) and got prepared. They put their guns and weapons on the table, Mia pulled up her sleeves, while Lila took off the cute pink-and-blue flower cardigan she was wearing. Underneath was a Red Poetoes shirt. Finally, they took off their shoes and took their positions.

"Five," started Mia.

"Four," continued Lila.

"Three,"

"Two,"

"One....."

"ZERO!!" they both shrieked as Lila started running towards Mia.

She came zooming in like a rocket ship on full speed, Mia dodged and gave a kick from the side. It went straight into Lila's hip, making Lila double up and clutch her hips.

It gave Mia time to attack back. She did a special lunge-punch called *oi-zuki* in karate. Lila saw that coming and immediately jump-dodged and landed on Mia, flooring her. Mia front-kicked her off and jumped back up.

Lila back-kicked Mia which is called *ushiro-geri* in special karate language. It hit Mia right on the bum. Screaming, she turned around quickly and did a random ju-jitsu kick. It landed on Lila's chest. And while Lila howled in pain, Mia did some more strikes, she kicked her elbows and punched her stomach.

Lila got really mad and did a some kind of spinning kick, or round kick or *mawashi geri* I should say. It made Mia go flying to the floor, and while Mia was trying to get up, Lila took hold of Mia's legs and started bashing them on the floor. Mia quickly did a backwards roll and landed on Lila's feet, making her trip. She landed on her back and Mia jumped on her and did a spear-hand (thrust) called *nukite* in Lila's face. Lila did a low, kung-fu kick right in Mia's knee.

While Mia held her knee, Lila did some leopard kung-fu moves such as low kicks, elbows and forearm strikes. Mia got bashed right against the wall. She had a big pain in her back but ignored it and did her special cart-wheel kick. Mia is quite tall, so her feet landed on Lila's head. Lila felt dizzy and collapsed to the floor.

By now a small crowd were watching. Some going like 'Ow!' or 'Owch!' or "Ooooh!' every time somebody went falling to the floor or did a cool move. They 'Ooooohed' and 'Ahhhhhhed' their heads off when Mia did her cart-wheel kicks, and when Lila did her special spinning-by-the-feet trick.

Lila shook her head quickly and got up. She dived to Mia's legs and with all her strength, lifted Mia by the legs and started spinning her around in circles. Mia screamed, before landing on the floor with a thud. More 'Ooooooooohs' and 'Ahhhhhhhhhhs'.

Mia got up quickly, shaking her head and calmly stared at Lila. Lila had very, very blue eyes. Like an angel's eyes. Except, this angel was a devil inside. Lila stared back. Mia had dark green eyes. Witch's eyes. Mia actually wanted to be a witch. She thinks they're cool, with their black cats and ability to fly anywhere on just a broomstick and their dark capes and hats and spells and potions. She always wished she was a witch. But she was just Mia. Mia with her brown hair, tied in a ponytail and the green eyes and a plain Red Potatoes shirt with shorts. Just a normal human being.

They were both staring at each other deeply now. Lila, angel-eyes glaring, Mia, witch-eyes widening.

Then suddenly Mia attacked. Quickly, like a leopard, she ran towards Lila at full speed. It was one of her famous tricks. She'd distract her opponent with a staring-contest, then quickly ran towards them and attack. It was a very clever trick. And always worked.

Lila, quite taken by surprise, opened her mouth to scream, but Mia was quicker. She jumped on Lila, making both of them fall. She used her long nails to scratch her. Then full on slapped Lila while also punching her stomach. Lila howled and tried to get up, but couldn't. Mia, put her foot under Lila's back, and lifted her. She was so strong because she worked out every day and visited the gym all the time. The gym had become part of her so named the gym Gerald. Gerald the Gym. So, she lifted Lila on her feet and spun her around before dropping her, face-first.

Even more 'Oooooohs' and 'Ahhhhhhs'.

Lila felt so sore. Her flawless skin was red. She tried attacking Mia some more, doing a few carless kicks and silly slaps. But Mia was ready for her. She either dodged, blocked or kicked Lila back, harder. Lila kept on falling and tripping. Her teeth were even bleeding now. So were her knees. And arms and legs and toes. Mia expected her to give up.

But Lila was mad. Very mad. In fact, so mad she could've ripped a human's head, right off their neck. That is what she wished she could do to Mia. So that's what's she tried. She suddenly got up and punched Mia right in the face. She kicked and kicked and kicked until Mia's knees and toes started bleeding. She picked Mia right up and threw her on the floor with all her power. She stamped on Mia's chest and stomach while Mia tried fighting back. She managed a few punches and kicks, but Lila was doing most of the work here. Mia was thrown here, thrown there, kicked here, kicked there, punched here, punched there, slapped here, slapped there.

On one throw, Lila clenched her fists as Mia hit the wall. She gritted her teeth and said, "You've always been a tough nut Badger, but you **CAN'T** get the better of me. You don't dare hurt me, or I'll come straight back, haunting you,"

"YOU SHUT UP!" shouted Mia and got up but was pushed back down. With an even louder thud.

Mia lay there, close to tears. She felt the biggest pain you could ever feel. Like as you'd been shot and got burnt by fire and fell off a bike all at the same time. Her arms and legs and elbows and toes and feet and neck and knees and head and chest and stomach all hurt. *I know you feel the biggest pain ever at the moment, but will you just let Miss High and Mighty Harty Fart win you? NO! Course not! You're a Badger! You can't and WON'T let that happen!*

And as Mia said those words in her head, she jumped up suddenly and ran for Lila. Slaps, punches, kicks, nudges, pushes, elbows, cart wheel kicks and spins were all included in what happened next. In short, Lila was completely destroyed. On the floor bleeding and crying, lay a very tear-faced Lila. Mia had won, it was obvious.

"Gimme dem clues now Hart, we had a deal!" Lila complained but eventually handed them over.

Mia was bruised, had a lot of cuts and bleeds and scrapes, but she felt good. Another three clues for the family! She had a look.

What starts with 'p' ends with 'e' and has a thousand letters in it?

And

And

DON'T MIND ME, IM JUST A RANDOM
PIECE OF PAPER

Well, actually, another TWO clues for the family.

13
CATCHING UP

It was eight o'clock in the evening. Day one was finally up. Everybody collected themselves back to their safe zones. Frank and Andrew and Leo and Harry and Mia and Jess and Tess and Cara saw lots and lots of people trying to get to their safe zones. They were like a big swarm of bees, desperate to get into their hives. And these bees were not allowed to kill or attack or even take out a weapon after eight pm.

Frank got to the safe zone first. Then Harry, then Mia, then Leo and Andrew, and then Tess, who came with Jess, and finally Cara. Oh wait, finally Chips. She arrived last, Sinister. Smith was already there. So were Dave and Jack.

"WELL, WELL. It's good to see all of you ALIVE, as I was not expecting that, ANYWAY let's get down to some business!" said Chips, rubbing her hands. Jack took on.

"Yes, yes as Chips said, I am on top of the moon to see you all here! Great! Now, I heard we got a few clues, mm?"

Tess and Harry and Andrew and Mia nodded.

"Fabulous! Now you, Tina, was it?" he asked.

"Tess," replied Tess.

"Oh yes, Tess. Now Tess, would you care to show us what you got?"

Tess took out her riddle that she found. Jack read it.

"My spine is stiff, my body is pale, I'm always ready to tell a tale. Oh yes, it's a book, isn't it?"

"Yes, I guessed that meant the library was a place for interesting clues, Chips and I headed there to find something, but we got held up a bit, and didn't manage to get there on time."

"Mm, well, you'll just have to go there tomorrow then, eh? Now, Harvey was it?"

"Harry," said Harry, sternly.

"Oh apologies, Harry, now I heard you may have been tricked into getting fake clues, mm?"

"Yes, it was The German Nightmares, they gave me a fake riddle, to confuse the team,"

"Ahh yes, now would you care to tell us the riddle?"

"Well of course, it says, 'I have hands, but no arms, a face but no eyes, what am I?' and by the way, the answer is a clock in case you didn't know,"

"Mm, I've seen a big grandfather clock in a room, they must be trying to make you think a clue was there,"

"Yeah, good point," said Harry, feeling a bit dumb.

"Moving on, now, what was it again? Andy, right?"

"Wrong, A-" before Andrew could finish Jack interrupted.

"Don't tell me! Alex? Alan? Alexander? Any of those right?'

"N-o-p-e. It's ANDREW," corrected Andrew.

"Oh right, Andrew, practically the same thing but whatever, I believe you have found a letter?"

"Correct, the letter is 'T',"

"Interesting, very interesting ……." He paused for a moment. "I have told very few of you, but I have a plan,"

"Well, it's not a 'plan' but it is very useful information," Jack continued, "I have discovered a secret room, in this tunnel. Lewis, purposely but it here, for somebody smart enough, to find. It has many, many clues. As you know, there are letters here that will probably spell out a phrase or sentence that will help win the riches. Nobody knows how many letters there are. Nobody apart from us. In the room, it said there is precisely twenty-four letters, so, when we get all twenty-four letters, we can try and work out what it says,"

"And I've found out, the number of riddles put out, thirty. But some people won't NEED all thirty. Some people may be able to work it out from ten or fifteen, you never know. And there are trails that lead to clues or landmarks that might include something interesting. These are stones, stuck with mega-triple-double-multi-super-super-spectacular-glue on the floor, so nobody can take them off. And it has said in the room, five places where you could find a trail. I believe there is more. But knowing where five is, is still really good!

Dave gave Jack a look. He obviously wanted Jack to add something else.

"FINE, Dave actually helped get this, so basically he did as much as me," added Jack. Then everyone started patting Dave's back and said stuff like, 'Good lad Dave!' and 'Good job, mate!' and 'Way to go dude!' and it irritated Jack. He immediately moved on.

"ANYWAY, now, Mina is it?"

"OH MY GOD IT'S MIA!" Mia said with a sigh. This guy obviously couldn't remember anyone's name. It was really annoying. He probably forgot his own name sometimes. "What's *YOUR* name?" she added.

"Jake – err - I mean Jack. Anyway, Mia, oh yes, now Mia, could you tell us what you found?"

"CERTAINLY. First, a letter 'E'. Secondly, a riddle, 'What starts with 'P' ends with 'E' and has a thousand letters in it?' The answer is a post office I'm guessing,"

"And you have guessed right. I'm nearly sure I've seen something that said 'POST OFFICE (NO ACTUAL POST OR MAIL. GO ASK ROYAL MAIL FOR SOMETHING LIKE THAT)' so a clue must be hidden there,"

"The sign, Simone?" asked Cara.

"Yes indeed! I need to introduce you to her. If you're the first agency she meets, you will probably be her favourite!"

"GOODY!!" shouted Jess, which sounds like something she'd say.

"Now you've all been amazing. Get a good night's sleep and wake up fresh in the morning for more. Me and Dave will come, at like, six o'clock or something.

We always will! So, you will get used to it! And if I were you, I'd have an early night!"

"OKAY JACK!" a few people said. (Jess, Tess, Harry, Leo and Andrew to be precise!)

"Night then!" said Jack and Dave.

"Nighttt Jackk anddd Davveee,"

they said, all suddenly sleepy.

And with that, they left.

14
A CHANCE TO DANCE

Days passed but they found nothing interesting. However, on day ten, Leo woke up at 5:57 am. He looked at his digital clock and knew either the men from yesterday (also known as the men from day one) or Jack or Dave would be there soon. In exactly two minutes and thirty-eight seconds, wait no, thirty-seven, thirty-six, thirty-five.. you get the point, they'd be there. He tried to open his eyes wider, he felt a bit sweaty. He knew he should've wore his summer pyjamas. What was he doing, wearing big, heavy winter pjyamas in the middle of August?

He looked at the time again, it read 5:59 am. *Maybe I should get dressed and make me a bowl of cereal. Then I'd be the first ready!*

Not if I get there first!

Frank was also awake. Staring at Leo, smiling. Leo smiled back, and they both got up and dashed quickly to the suitcase where they left all their clothes.

Look, look, look, look ....

AHA! Leo Brooks! Leo quickly put his t-shirt on while Frank was still looking for his. Then, **"GOT IT!!"**

Frank Johnson! He put his shirt on in precisely 1.78 seconds and started on his shorts. Leo was putting on his socks, trying to hurry.

When they both finally finished (Leo finished first, in case you're interested) they quickly got the muesli box and started pouring into the bowls clumsily. Frank fetched two spoons from a random suitcase and they started eating. They had got dressed and began eating in only four seconds. A record.

It turned six o'clock. And in the exact same second, there was a loud bang. It was the door being opened of course. This time by Jack, Dave, two different guards and a woman.

"Wakey Wake- oh! Somebody's up early!" said Dave in his usual jolly voice.

"Mornin' Dave and Jack and you, mysterious lady!" they both replied.

"Mysterious lady! You give me the chuckles young Frank and young Leo! This is Simone!" said Jack.

Everybody was starting to wake up. Apart from Harry of course. Chips and Mia and Jess and Andrew and Sinister. Smith were now wide awake.

"OH! Hi then Simone!" said Leo and Simone laughed. She had bright blue eyes and blonde hair and was wearing a blue-suit dress with a name tag that said;

Simone Elliot
Design & Room Manager

With a picture on the side with her face.

"Looks like I'm a bit early to meet my potatoes!" she laughed. She had a beautiful laugh. It made you smile, no matter how you were feeling. Cross, depressed, anxious, you name it.

"No, no! Not at all! We're all just a bit lazy …" said Chips as she got up and rubbed her eyes.

Soon, when they were all dressed and ready, they started chatting to Simone.

"So, are you da famous Simone, Dave keeps talking about? I'm your biggest FANN!!" lisped Jess, cuddling Mr. Scruffles, her teddy.

"Awww, you're so sweet! Yes, I'm Simone, do you like the signs I made?"

There was a loud 'YES' as the children were all desperate to get Simone's attention.

They asked lots of questions such as;

"How old are you?"

"How did you end up working here?"

"Who is your best friend?"

"Are you rich?"

"Are you married?"

"Do you like animals?"

"Does my breath smell like muesli?"

And she'd answer with things like;

"I'm twenty, pet!"

"My Dad, used to work here, so I guess he made me join!"

"Best friend, eh? Well, I'm friends with most of my fellow employees, and perhaps we could grow to become friends too, eh?" there was a loud 'YES' to this too.

"Not rich, but I have a reasonable salary so I'm about average!"

"No, I'm single at the moment!"

"I love them! I use to have a pet parrot when I was young. And I loved going to the zoo!"

"Well, you've just eaten some, so I'm guessing so!"

After a load of questions, laughs and chats, Jack suddenly said, "Now, settle down everybody, I'm glad everyone seems to be enjoying Si's visit, but now I have important information to share with you all," he said, "Today, they are hosting an activity called 'A Chance Too Dance'. We have not found a single clue in the past nine days (apart from the trails) so this is our opportunity to get something. Only a certain number of agencies are allowed to participate, so we need to go out at exactly eight o'clock and head straight to the-"

"-THE DYING ROOM (NO ROOM FOR LIVING HERE)!" chirped in Simone.

"Yes, thank you Simone, that is exactly it. Now, in this Chance to Dance, agencies will be competing in dance competitions. People will get eliminated with time, and first place, gets three clues. Second place get two, and third gets one. So, we will try our best. Any keen dancers here?"

Instead of being met by the deadly silence he expected, a few hands went up, they were Jess, Tess, Frank, Cara, Harry and even Sinister. Smith!

"Oh, not bad! Is that it, any others?" asked Jack.

They all looked at Chips. Memories of her dancing with the mop and the cat started rushing into their heads. A few people even sniggered.

Jack followed their gaze and looked at Chips too, "Well, well Chips! Are **YOU** a keen dancer? Because according to the children, it seems so to me!"

Chips went red before saying, "No, no! These children have the audacity to-" but before Chips was about to say, whatever she was going to say, Frank turned on the radio to My Heart Will Go On as it was the only one, he could remember Chips dancing to.

Chips got up quickly and started her old-fashioned, elegant dancing. Jack and Dave and Simone and even the two officer-guards seemed taken by surprise. The children were trying not to laugh as they watched Chips dance around on her own planet. Planet Chips.

Out of nowhere, the familiar black CAT jumped onto the stage and joined Chips. This time with a pair of neon BLUE sunglasses.

After many, many, many songs, Cara decided that enough was enough and turned off the radio. Chips looked at them. "What are you staring at??" she wanted to know.

"Err …. okay … I guess Chips IS a keen dancer then. That's sorted! I think … ANYWAY, you will all have to dance anyway, but it's good to have some keen dancers …. And …. WHOA, LOOK AT THE TIME! In exactly three minutes we will all head straight to The Dying Room where The Chance To Dance is being held!"

"Who is it held by?" asked Tess.

"A man who works for Richard Lewis called Felix Henderson. He is Lewis's loyal friend, so Lewis always trusts Felix!"

The familiar ring, rang in their ears.

RINGGGG - RINGGG - RINGGGGGG

"RUN, RUN, RUN!!!" shrieked Jack and they all ran at full speed towards The Dying Room.

In exactly one minute and thirty-six seconds, they had arrived. They had to leave any weapons they had at the door. (Felix didn't want any drama) When they arrived, they seen another four agencies there. The Globs, Marshmallow City, Takeaway Timers and another agency they didn't know.

Jack went over to Felix. They chatted a bit, and then Jack came back and said, "Felix said only fifteen agencies are allowed to participate. Only another ten now!"

After a few seconds came The Toilet Nails, then The German Nightmares, after them, The Sassy Grannies. Few minutes later, another agency they didn't know. After, came Chocolate World.

"YAY!!" said Jess. The Red Potatoes and Chocolate World were firm friends.

Seconds after, Creepy Crawlies, West Coast and Aliens 'n' America came. Only two more.

Wannabe Bears arrived. One more.

One more

One more

One more

One more

One more …

After a long while. Came the Red Poetoes.

"**NOOOOOOOOOOOOOOOO!!**" screamed the whole of Red Potatoes.

"Calm down everybody! Now, Welcome to *A Chance To Dance!* There will be CHALLENGES and COMPETITIONS and 𝒟𝒜𝒩𝒞𝒾𝒩𝒢! You are all very lucky to be here, because there are some 𝒫𝑅𝒥𝒵𝑬𝒮! Now, the teams participating are, **The Globs and** Marshmallow City and Takeaway Timers and 𝓡𝒶𝓋𝑒𝓃𝓈 and **THE RED POTATOES AND** *The Toilet Nails and* The German Nightmares and The Sassy Grannies and Thomas The Tank Engine Fans and Chocolate World and Creepy Crawlies and *West Coast and* Aliens 'n' America and **Wannabe Bears and** The Red Poetoes! Lots of lovely agencies! Now, in dance and ballroom, every dancer has a profession nickname, I want you all too think of one for yourselves and let me know when you have thought of one so we can start the challenges!" said Felix.

Nicknames, eh? This was The Red Potatoes' specialty. Thinking of funny names and nicknames. That's how they got their name.

Precisely two minutes later, everybody had thought of a name.

"Now, I'm going to ask everybody for their name. I'll say mine first. My name is Jackay West. Now, you Chips!" said Jack.

"Mine is Hot Chip," replied Chips.

"Lovely, next!"

"Sweetie Stevie."

"Nice! Didn't expect that coming from you, Mr. Smith!" chuckled Jack.

"Mine's Dazey Doo," said Dave.

"Okay, next, keep going,"

"Franko Mousse!"

"Tres Lee-Oh!"

"Andro Jem!"

"Harick Stylez!"

"Mimi Gaze!"

"Jas Queen!"

"Teeeez Tearz!"

"Crabay Pattay!"

"Wow! This agency is more creative than I thought! Harick Stylez! Jas Queen! Tres Lee-Oh! Even better than the grown-ups!"

"Ahem!" coughed Chips.

"Oh! Let's not forget Hot Chip!"

"That's what I thought!" huffed Chips.

"Excuse me everyone! That should be *enough* time now! I shall ask you all for your 'names' now!" said Felix, "I shall start with **The Globs** and will go on and on and on…."

After four agencies, it was the Red Potatoes' turn.

"……………RED POTATOES! Let's start with the S.H.M, Jack Spurs!"

"Thank you, Felix, my nickname is Jackay West!"

Felix wrote it down. "Great! Now, Dave, the S.H.A, what is yours?"

"Mine is Dazey Doo!"

More writing. "Nice! Now Red Potatoes' manager, Chips I believe, care to tell us yours?"

"Yes, mine is Hot Chip," said Chips sternly.

Felix wrote did down as he chuckled. "Very creative! Now Red Potatoes' +1 adult. Steven Smith!"

"I'm Sweetie Stevie." Replied Sinister. Smith casually, as if he hadn't just said the most hilarious thing in the world.

The laughter was unbelievable. All kinds of laughs were to be heard. Fake laughs, high-pitched laughs, lovely laughs, loud laughs, quiet laughs, giggle laughs, chuckle laughs, screaming laughs. In short, What Sinister. Smith just said, was so hilarious the whole room was laughing.

Writing. "Very, very, VERY creative if I do say Mr. Smith! Now, the agents- who-err- are children, may say theirs. I will call out a name and that person will tell me their nickname. Frank Johnson," called out Felix.

"Franko Mousse!" * laughter *

Writing again. "Leo Brooks,"

"Tres Lee-Oh!" * Lots of laughter *

Even more writing, "Andrew Smith,"

"Andro Jem!" * laughter *

Writinggggg, "Harry Peters,"

"Harick Stylez!!" * Lots and lots of laughter *

More writing, "Mia Badger,"

"Mimi Gaze!" * Small laughter *

w-r-i-t-i-n-g, "Jess badger,"

"JAS QUEEN!" * Laughter and more laughter *

Yep, you guessed it, writing, "Tess Garcia,"

"Teeez Tearz!" * Average laughter *

Ugh, too much writing, "And finally, Cara Michaels,"

"Crabay Pattay!" * Deffo more than average laughter! *

"Well, thank you Red Potatoes, now, moving on to--"

AFTER MANY, MANY, MANY AND ONE MORE MANY AGENCIES LATER

"...... AND THAT WAS OUR LAST AGENCY! Now, let the competitions begin!!" shouted Felix and then some random trumping noise was heard.

"**CHALLENGE 1:** *Dance, Dance, Dance!* Two people will be picked from two different agencies, and they will both have dance, and they will both be rated by a panel of judges and the person with the lowest score, is ELIMINATED. BUT, fear not! If you are eliminated, it doesn't mean your **TEAM** is eliminated, just you. If first place was on Thomas the Tank Engine Fans for example, they win. But if to say, Harick Stylez from Red Potatoes was eliminated that just decreases your team's chances of winning because you are a person short! Everybody understands?"

There was a general 'Yes' but a few people said 'No' but Felix didn't explain again.

"Now!" he looked at his paper, "TIMMY and Mikz Sik are to compete first! Come on onto the stage you two!"

One boy about thirteen and one man about forty came onto the stage.

"Now, we shall start with TIMMY. The theme for the dance is ballet. You are expected to follow the theme, if you don't, you lose points. You have two minutes, TIMMY. Off you go!" said Felix in that cheerful, loud voice of his.

Relaxing ballet music was put on and all eyes were on TIMMY. TIMMY's real name was actually Thomas Mitchell. He was very famous and very good at his job. Thomas was good at almost everything. He played sports including golf and ice hockey and skiing. He did dance, including hip-hop and rock and BALLET. He was good at missions, he was stealthy, strong and wise. So, if anyone could win this, it was Ravens' Thomas Mitchell.

TIMMY (I may as well call him by his nickname) stood on his tiptoes, eyes closed and hands high. As soon as the music tune changed a bit, he walked slowly and gently before stopping, and lifting one of his legs backwards, arms stretched to his sides. More movement and prancing and dancing. It was obvious this boy was a talented ballet dancer. He ending his solo with a handstand, and then stood up straight, hands up high. Clapping. Mostly from Ravens.

"Lovely solo! The judges will now show their scores!" said Felix

One judge did an eight. The second a seven. Third a nine. Forth, was also a nine. Fifth was an eight.

"Great score! Now, Mikz Sik, the stage is yours!"

Mikz Sik was Mick Stevens. He was an amazing spy and agent, but a worthless dancer. He worked at the Toilet Nails.

He did a few twirls (clumsy) and even attempted a few handstands and cartwheels. NOTE; they did

NOT end up well. He mostly just landed on his bottom or back. The music finished and nearly did Mikz Sik's life. He lay there, embarrassed and sore. Hardly any claps, not even from The Toilet Nails.

"Well, it could have been worse! Let's see what the JUDGES have to say!"

The judges were NOT impressed. Judge one rated two. Judge two rated three. Judge three rated one. Judge four must have felt bad for Mikz Sik, because he rated four. And judge five rated a three.

"OK, interesting scores from the judges! Thirteen! Good score but NOT good enough to get through to the next round. Mikz Sik, you are ELIMINATED!" said Felix dramatically. After all, his whole life was practically theatre!

Mikz Sik left the room, embarrassed and miserable.

"Okay folks, next two people are ….. DUN, DUN, DUNNNNN! Bug Time and Ellis Broos!"

Bug Time won. So did Jam Tart. And Scarl Piratez. And Bun Av. And Becz Boo-Boo. AND Lilz Stinkz. The Red Potatoes got MEGA bored watching others dance and have fun. That is, until, it was their turn.

"………. AND NEXT UP, I SHALL HAVE ….. TRES LEE-OH AND MWAH BE!"

"LEO, LEO! IT'S YOUR TURN!!" screamed the whole of The Red Potatoes.

Leo was up against a boy called Matt Bennet. Another child who was thirteen. A boy called Matt Bennet that was a totally show off and was so full of himself. A boy called Matt Bennet that worked for The

100

Globs. Leo would need to try his very best if he wanted to win this.

"Mwah Be, you can go first. The theme here is rock and roll. Here is a guitar and some speakers, you will be creating your own music as you 𝒟𝒜𝒩𝒞𝐸!" said Felix.

Mwah Be took the guitar (a heavy metal red one) and got up to the stage. Lots of people starting clapping for no reason. Maybe it was because they knew Mwah Be. Or maybe they just thought him really handsome.

He started a few notes as he put his head down. Then the music started getting louder and his head starting getting higher, until his head and the music couldn't have got higher.

He started walking around the stage, head high, hands on guitar. A professional.

He did a few moves here and there, his face matching the sound of the music. And every now and then, he'd wink at the audience, making them go mad, as if he was a professional musician that came to play at a school concert or something.

At moments, he'd jazz it up by doing a shake or wriggle or just a cool move. He was fire. And the whole audience were under his spell.

The whole audience apart from, of course, The Red Potatoes. They were totally unfazed and unimpressed. Every single member of The Red Potatoes, was staring at Mwah Be as if they wanted to spit at his stupid, smug ugly face.

Mwah Be kept on dancing and shaking and playing the guitar, making his face expressions change at every different note. He looked as if he'd been doing this his whole life.

A little before two minutes, the noise started getting quieter and quieter and he stopped with a grin and his hands held out high. Leo half expected the whole audience to start throwing roses at him or something. The rest of the agency saw the look on Leo's face.

"It's alright Leo, you can do much better!" said Mia.

"Yeah, show them what Tres Lee-Oh can do!" comforted Frank.

"Get out there and just try your best!" cheered Cara

"Yeah!"

"Yes sir!"

"Come on!"

"You can do it!"

"YA YOU CANN! Maybe you would wike a jammie dodger to cheer you up?" said Jess, smiling at him, with a gap in her front teeth. It was hard to believe she was actually ten.

"Thanks Jess- err I mean, Jas Queen, but I think I'll pass!" replied Leo.

"*WHAT A GREAT PERFORMANCE!!* That was BRILLIANT! Let's see what the judges think!!" said Felix.

Some of the judges actually thought it hard to share his enthusiasm. Richard Lewis mostly hired

102

people that were not snobs. Most of them thought Mwah Be a snob, and didn't like him much. But a judge is a judge, they had to be fair.

Judge one rated eight. Judge two rated seven. Judge three rated nine. Judge four voted eight. AND judge five voted nine.

"*Lovely* scores! Let's see if Tres Lee-Oh can beat this! Come on up Tres Lee-Oh! Let us see what you have to offer!!"

"COME ON LEO!!" shouted the whole of Red Potatoes.

Leo took his guitar and got up onto the stage. He stared at the audience. They stared back, waiting for him to start, or do something. Then Leo's eyes turned to The Red Potatoes. They were staring at him, in a comforting sort of way. He stared at them more. He just knew he couldn't let them down, after all they have done for him.

He put on a random pair of sunglasses and started. Elegant but rock notes started coming out of the guitar. Leo thought to himself, *wow! I'm actually playing a guitar!* His notes started getting higher, then lower, then higher, then lower. Until he stayed on the same level and tune.

'Yeah, I'm gonna rock and roll!' sang Leo, making up a song to get him more points. He danced as he sang.

'And I'm gonna haunt your soul! Yeah yeah!'

'You better watch out,' he continued.

'When I'm out and about!' he then gave the audience a big, fat smile. Leo, (I mean, Tres Lee-oh!)

was having the absolute best time of his life. He was singing, rocking and rolling and dancing! His body moves and vibrates as the music goes on, making up his own lines and smiling and winking. He was amazing. Almost as good as Mwah Be. No, *better.*

'This rock is making me go blind!'

'Please don't mind me cuz I'm losin' my mind!' he said this last line and his music got really loud before dropping, into an intense silence.

"*That was fablastical!* You boy have got some talent! Let's see what the judges' thoughts are!" said Felix.

Judge one rated ten. Judge two rated six. Judge three rated nine. Judge four rated seven. And before judge five rated everybody in the hall gasped. It was the exact same as Mwah Be's so far! If judge five voted less the nine, Leo would be eliminated.

"OOOOOOOOOH   OOOOOOOOOOOOOH OOOOOOOOOOOOOOH! This is very interesting! This last score depends on who is going to win! Cross your fingers and toes everybody! This is going to be *EXCITING!*"

The audience fell quiet as judge five, (his name was actually Barry) wrote down his score. Leo and the whole entire Red Potatoes crossed their fingers and toes like Felix recommended, they hoped and wished, wished and hoped that they would win. Jess even prepared a Jammie Dodger for Leo. They'd all be devastated if Leo lost.

Judge five finally finished. He held his rate up high, proud. It was a ten.

The whole of Red Potatoes and Chocolate World (they were friends) and anybody else that liked or weren't enemies with The Red Potatoes cheered. They stood up high and screamed,

"HOORAY!"

Leo was so happy he didn't even know how to act. He wanted to cry, laugh, jump with joy, twirl, scream. Mwah Be, looked absolutely horrified. How could they miss his sweet moves?? He glared at Leo and stuck his tongue out, jealous. Leo rolled his eyes and stuck his tongue back. And mouthed 'Jealous snob!' at him.

Then Leo went off the stage, the red velvet curtains swaying as he ran past. He headed straight to the Red Potatoes. A few people said 'Well done, Tres Lee-Oh!' as he went past. Others patted his back. But Leo wasn't paying attention.

"LEO!!" yelled Frank as Leo appeared from the crowd. He ran over and hugged him and said "That wasn't half bad mate! Where did ya learn dem cool moves, eh?"

The others ran over and joined them, giving Leo hugs and words of congratulations and thanks and good job.

"LEO THAT WAS GREAT!"

"GOOD JOB!"

"TEACH ME HOW YOU DID THAT!!"

"YOU WERE ROCKING OUT THERE!"

"THAT PERFORMANCE WAS FAB!"

"DO YOU WANT A JAMMIE DODGER??"

Leo thanked them and hugged them as Chips, Jack and Dave came over.

"That was absolutely wonderful, Leo! I am so proud of you!" said Chips giving him a hug.

"You were on fire out there! Nice lyrics! You were class, good job!" Jack said.

Dave gave him a hug and a lollipop. Apple flavour. His absolute favourite. Leo looked down at it, surprised. "I know everything! Maybe that History Room taught me a thing or two, but apart from that, I still know everything!" said Dave.

Leo laughed, he felt so happy. He never ever has felt so proud. He was not eliminated, and his team were proud of him. Life was *sweet*.

Many, many rounds passed by. The Red Potatoes got lots of other goes, Andrew and Tess were eliminated, but only by close. Mainly because Tess was so nice, that when Lerta Star (Loretta King) glared at her and said, "You better let *me* win!" Tess actually tried her best to not do her best. And the Lerta ended up winning by four points. Andrew was useless at dancing, but he absolutely put his effort into it. Leaping and jumping and dancing and trying. But his best wasn't good enough to win. Few more points and he WOULD have won. Harry, Mia, Chips and Dave had a go, and they all won. So, things weren't too bad.

"**CHALLENGE 2:** *dancing statues!* Fifty out of the two hundred and ten are eliminated, so it's time for a new challenge! This is basically musical statues, just you have to dance to the theme you are given. If you move, you are eliminated. There will be five rounds, so, good luck everyone! The theme is K-Pop, music is on in three …. two …. one!"

Just as he said that, a man called Bill, turned on the music to K-Pop. Some staff members used jet-pack thingies to fly up to the ceiling to be able to check that everybody was doing the right thing.

Everybody was dancing to the K-Pop like there was no tomorrow. Some people were even singing, even if there was no need to.

CLICK the music was turned off after ten minutes. Some people weren't quick enough and when the music stopped, they stopped seconds after. Some people moved because they were in such a position that was so uncomfortable, they couldn't help a little move. They couldn't help being eliminated either.

Then the music was turned back on, this time to ballroom. Some people already started dancing to the K-Pop they were expecting. So, they were ELIMINATED.

Ballroom was Chips' specialty. She knew how to prance and dance and leap peacefully all over the place. Same with Ballet. Chips started, and a few people looked at her, hypnotised. The Red Potatoes, unlike their manager, were terrible at Ballroom. They tried to copy some of Chips' moves, but they didn't quiteeeeeee master it.

Dave was surprisingly good. He could twirl and leap, he almost did as good as Chips!

"OOOOOOOH! Take a look at *Hot Chip* and *Dazey Doo!* Those are some sweet skills!" said Felix enthusiastically.

Some more people stared. At both Chips *and* Dave. They looked like total experts. Professional dancers. The Red Poetoes stared the most. Not in an admiring way. In a jealous way of course. They were glaring at them, a glare a cat does before it pounces.

Lila Hart (or should I say, Lil Princess, as that's her stupid nickname?!) was staring too of course. Staring mainly at Mia, her deadliest enemy. Mia didn't actually care; she was just dancing. Trying her best to not lose. And, fair for Mia, she actually did OK. Not bad. At least not bad enough to lose.

On the other side, Frank was really struggling. He had literal NO idea how to *Ballroom* dance. So, sadly, three minutes into the round of *Ballroom*, he got eliminated. A smile creeped up on one of Red Poetoes agents, Theez Co (Theo Turners). Because Frank was HIS enemy.

CLICK. The music stopped once more. Even though some of them were really into their dance, all of The Red Potatoes stopped quickly. Sinister. Smith (or shall I say, Sweetie Stevie!) was in an awkward position, but they knew he'd manage to hold it for a bit longer. Sixteen people couldn't hold THEIR positions, so they got, you know by now, eliminated.

Mia was holding her breath as she stared at Lila. She badly, **badly** wanted that pathetic, cry-baby, wimpy, poop-faced, girlie-pearly to get eliminated.

But sadly, she didn't.

The music was put back on, this time, the theme was *Hip Hop*.

The dancing continued. Three or four people got eliminated as they started dancing to *Ballroom* instead of *Hip Hop*. Thankfully for The Red Potatoes, they were much better at *Hip Hop* then *Ballroom*.

It was no problem for Chips, as, luckily for her, she could dance to any music.

Simone (Simmy Boo-Boo) was dancing with some kids along the way. Even some adults. She mostly danced with Jess, but sometimes it would be the occasional dark, tall stranger or the mysterious, long figure or the cheerful, sunny lady or even the spoiled, killer child.

Jess didn't exactly **MIND** when Simone danced with someone else (even if she wanted her to herself. Jess is like that you know!) but when Simone danced with Pamela Walls (Pammy Pie), Jess's arch enemy (another cute, tiny ten year old, who still played with teddies and likes biscuits) things got SERIOUS.

Simone randomly let go of Jess and started dancing on her own for two seconds, before she swiftly but elegantly twirled towards Pamela's area and held her hand and started dancing with her. This got Jess absolutely raging. How dare Simone go over to that total SPOILED BRAT! She was dancing with her now, they were both giggling, well, I'll show them, she thought.

So then, she **HIP-HOPPED** over to them and with all her strength, jumped up and kicked Pamela on her shoulders/neck area. Pamela screamed and fell down, face first. Simone gasped. Pamela started crying and looked up and saw Jess. She glared at her through her tears while Jess stood, smirking. A big, smug smirk.

Pamela jumped up (shoulders and a bit of her neck bleeding because Jess was wearing her big red boots) and at the exact same time,

CLICK. Music turned off again.

Pamela was running towards Jess when the music stopped, so she got **ELIMINATED** for moving.

Pamela stuck her tongue out at Jess as she walked towards the door, her curly, black stuck onto her face because of tears. Another Red Poetoe eliminated. Life was SWEET.

Lots of people got eliminated on this round, some of them were famous agents, like Carlos Walters (yes him again! His nickname is Colo Polo), Alana Franks (Allo Foo), Paul Hornby (Papa Horn), Oliver Simons (Ollie Sausage) and Jane McKay (Janey Moo).

The Red Potatoes managed to hold their breath and made it to round four. The second last round. The theme was *Line Dancing*.

As soon as she could, Simone *line danced* towards Jess.

"You Potatoes are really tough! Why do you hate her so much, eh? She's a lovely girl!" said Simone, as she continued *Line Dancing*.

"No, she's not! She's a weal DEVIL! She's really mean to me. She's just a disgusting ogre. I HATE HER!

Go away Simone! Go find another Pamela to dance with!" said Jess so seriously that Simone wondered if she was actually talking to Jess. Jess soon flounced off when she finished her speech.

Simone sighed, she just wanted everyone to get on. It was a big shame, because Jess had been really fun and energetic.

Ah well, I'm sure I'll get round her. Why does Jess have to make a big deal? Thought Simone.

Most of The Red Potatoes were struggling on this theme. *Line Dancing*. In fact, even Chips was finding it hard. She worried she'd get eliminated.

Two got eliminated on this one. It was Jack and Mia (it was okay, because Lila got eliminated too, so Mia didn't take on heart). After all, *Line Dancing*, was not the Red Potatoes' specialty.

Cara was doing her best. She was moving a lot, so she ended up with random groups of people. In one of the groups Cara was in, she saw Simone.

"Why you looking so down, Si? Wassup?" she asked, as she continued *Line Dancing*.

Simone smiled when Cara called her 'Si'. It was a nickname, she absolutely *loved* being called.

"Nothing, it's just Jess is mad at me, and I'm not even one hundred percent sure why!" she replied.

"Oh dear, that's very unusual and unexpected, Jess is probably having one of her little moodies. How did it happen though?"

"I was dancing with a random child, by the name Pamela, and I don't think Jess took a shine to her, so she kicked her with them big, red boots! Then I asked her why she didn't like her, and that she was a lovely girl, so she had a go at me, saying she was a devil and I had no sense and go find yourself a Pamela girl or something. So that's how it happened," explained Simone.

"Oh, I see, Pamela Walls is actually Jess's deadliest enemy! Fancy you pick her out of all the children in the room! But I know how to get her. Write her a special note, and I'll give it to her, if I can find her," offered Cara.

"Okay! I'll do that now," replied Simone as she got out a random piece of paper and started writing.

When she gave it to Cara it said this,

Dearest Jess,

I apologize for my unappreciated behaviour, I should know better. That Pamela Walls was a right devil, indeed. She looks like a walking forest, with that big bushy hair of hers. She certainly has no taste, and I had no taste, dancing with that Wallsie-Ballsie, she is such a disappointment. More of an ogre then a girl! I think she should be locked up for trickery! You're much, much better!

Your friend, Simone.

"You're too nice! Writing an apology-note to that spoiled-brat that had a go at you for no real explanation! You're just to *kind!*" said Cara, as if she was insulting her.

She **Line danced** quickly over to Jess and handed her the note.

"Simone sent this," she said. Jess read the note and smiled. Finally, she was waiting for an apology!

Jess wrote a note back, gave it to Cara, who delivered it to Simone. Simone smiled as she read it, it said;

Dear Simone,

You should be sorry, very, very sorry actually. But maybe I was a bit to HARSH on you. How were you suppose to know that, that angel-looking devil was actually a human ogre? Nice joke by the way! I guess we can be friends again, as you are very funny and fun. Just please make sure you don't dance with anymore girlie looking baby children. Especially Pamela Walls kind of children! She is the worse, she is meaner and ruder and patheticer then any other child. Pamela Walls should deffo be locked up! So yeah, I'm running out of things to say.

Your friend Jess.

P.S this line dancing is so annoying and boring, make it stop!

So, there you are, the story of how Jess and Simone had a fight, and how they made up again, any complain letters about how boring the fight was, go straight to them, thank you very much.

CLICK. Another ten minutes up. One round left. And only one hundred and seventeen people left.

I mean one hundred and nine, as eight people moved when the music was off.

Chips and Dave and Cara and Jess and Leo and Harry were the only Red Potatoes left.

Harry had actually done very well for a boy who loved his sleep and had nightmares about his own socks haunting him. Especially the ones creeping out of toilets.

He had somehow survived,

Dance, dance, dance!

K-Pop dancing,

Ballroom dancing,

Hip Hop dancing,

Line Dancing andddd .....

*Music turned on*and we will see about Rock and Roll!

Rock and Roll was possibly The Red Potatoes' favourite one. They knew how it goes. Jess danced with Simone, Cara danced with her imaginary crabs, Leo and Harry did a dance together, Chips just danced by herself like there was no tomorrow, and Dave danced with anyone he could see.

The Red Potatoes were having the best time of their lives (that don't belong to them apparently!). And when I say The Red Potatoes, I mean *all* Red Potatoes. The ones in the tunnel and the ones still at the agency. Because, of course, they were still partying.

In the room there was precisely one hundred and nineteen people. Oh, actually, one hundred and *twenty.* Because apart from the one hundred and nine candidates, nine staff members and one producer called Felix, there was a rather *uninvited* guest. And they were watching everyone from their unknown hiding place. Or more specifically, watching the Red Potatoes-

CLICK. The last round had finished. And according to my calculations, only ninety-nine people were left. Including Chips and Dave and Harry and Leo and Cara and Jess.

"Challenge over! Great job to anyone who has not been ... umm ... **eliminated!**" said Felix cheerfully.

"**CHALLENGE 3**: *Musical Dancing Chairs!* In this challenge you will be basically playing musical chairs, but, last three standing (or sitting I should say!) will all have a chance to win first place! Or second or third obviously! So, *GOOD LUCK* everybody! But not too much luck, har, har!" said Felix as he chuckled at his own terrible joke.

Chips shook her head, the staff members here, obviously didn't know a good joke when they hear one.

Ninety-eight chairs had been set out for the ninety-nine contestants. The music was to be turned on in FIVE, FOUR, THREE, TWO, ONE ....

Music was turned on to the VERY familiar baby-shark-doo-doo-doo-doo. A few people chuckled, a few girls giggled in a sickly girlie way, some people

115

burst out laughing. This is until, Bill gave them

THE DEATH STARE OF DOOM

that said, 'Do not mock what songs I pick, I'm a professional and know what I'm doing!' and how do I know that? Because I read the latest copy of *One Million Bill Face Expression Meanings (useful) written by Bill himself.* It really is a useful book; I highly recommend it!

Anyway, forget the book-recommendation this is not *Book Recommending's For Young and Old Readers by Rose Upton* or *Good Books (including this one) by Professor Mayo Brown* or *For Goodness' Sake Help Me Find A Book! By Bruce Hill* which for your information, are really good books that I really recommend.

ANDDDDD I better shut up about

book recommendations now.

Now then, where was I? Ah yes, Bill put on the famous baby-shark thing and he gave them the expression look that said …. Well, you know, so now everybody is walking around the chairs, while singing baby-shark in their heads. (Can't blame them, it's a catchy song!)

Usually, you would stop half way through the song in musical chairs, but Bill was too engrossed with the song, he only stopped when the music finished, so many people were prepared.

The person who lost the first round was a very, and I mean very, dumb boy from Thomas The Tank Engine Fans. Did I actually say boy? He is actually a

116

baby. So is the rest of the team. The manager, boss thingy is a big, fat baby, who has red cheeks and can talk like a forty-year-old chimney sweep who stays up half the night. The dumb boy's (who isn't that dumb compared to his team that all got eliminated) name is Freddie Enright. (A.K.A Tiny Froddo)

The rest grabbed a chair almost immediately, while he was just standing there howling for England. He got eliminated and that was the end of Thomas The Tank Engine Fans.

Then the rounds continued and more and more people were getting eliminated. Bill played some of the following songs;

Twelve Days of Christmas, Baa-Baa Black Sheep, Twinkle Twinkle Little Star, MARY HAD A LITTLE LAMB, Barbie Girl and a lot of other kids' songs and stuff. (Please don't ask why)

Of course, Red Potatoes were not perfect as, in round twenty-four Jess got eliminated, and in thirty-six, Tres Lee-Oh walked the plank, then in thirty-nine Dave went bye-bye, after, in round sixty-four Hot Chip couldn't grab a chair, and much later, in round ninety, Harry was not quick enough. Only Cara remains. The fate of the Red Potatoes lays in Cara's crabby hands.

The remaining eight, apart from Cara, were Billie Carney (Bug Time, familiar, eh? Works for Ravens), Jen Green (Jam Tart, also familiar, eh? Works for Ravens), Rebecca Upton (Becks Biscuit, works for The Takeaway Timers), Emma Millar (Nice Creamy, also works for Ravens), Noah Hill (Clickoo, works for West Coast), Carl Cox (Catty Croc, works for The Globs),

Theo Turners (Theez Co, works for UGH, Red Poetoes) and finally, William Browne (Willz Killz, works for Marshmallow City). So, Cara was actually up against a BIG challenge.

Music on. To some weird Titanic song, I'm guessing. The game goes on and the children (ta-da! Only children are left, proves children are *much* better than adults!) cautiously walk around the eight chairs.

CLICK. Music is turned off. Cara thankfully manages to grab a seat. Willz Killz doesn't.

"SORRY TO SAY WILLZ KILLZ, BUT <u>YOU</u> ARE, **ELIMINATED!**" said Felix, as Willz runs out of the arena.

Music back on. This time to a very old song. So old that I'm not sure what song it even is (see, I'm not that old!) okay, I'd better stop saying the word 'old' now!

CLICK. Music off. Bye-Bye Catty Croc.

CLICK. Music on. Hello 'Rule Britannia'.

CLICK. Music off. Goodbye Becks Biscuit.

CLICK. Music on. Hello 'Mother'. (this one stays on for quite a while as Bill enjoys mouthing the words, *I am your mother!*)

CLICK. Music off. Goodbye Theez Co. (Cara thinks, *YESS!! NO MORE RED POOPOOTOES!)*

CLICK. Music on. Hello 'Green Green Grass'.

CLICK. Music off. So long Bug Time.

CLICK. Music on. Hello 'Shake It Off'. (This also stays on longer than usual, because Bill enjoys singing it)

Now. There is only four left. Two Ravens, one West Coast and One Red Potato. This was going to be interesting.

CLICK. Music off. Cara fortunately managed to get a seat. She took a big breath of relief.

From The Red Potatoes' safe zone, you could hear shrieks and shrieks of cheering. They had been watching the whole thing from a ninety-inch plasma TV. With buckets of popcorn.

Unfortunately for Jam Tart, it was bye-bye for her.

"OH MY FLUFFY KITTENS, WE HAVE FINALLY GOTTEN TO THE FINAL THREE!! amazing! Now, the final CHALLENGE IS; A DANCING TRIVIA! Hope you've got some good dancing knowledge, because THIS is the final test! BOB AND SAMMY, get these three fantastic people a pencil and some PAPER!'" shouted Felix, "ALL YOU WATCHING THIS ON THE TELEVISON BOX THINGY, will be absolutely blown away! This is the final test. Which one of you, will be winning THREE clues? And who's winning TWO and ONE? Will soon be REVEALED!"

Two men, by the names Bob and Sammy, got the three finalists a paper each and a pencil.

"Sir Alfred Carter, will be asking the questions, and trust ME, this guy is ALBERT EINSTEIN!"

A tall, thin man came out of the darkness. He had a brown moustache and glasses. He was wearing a bow tie.

"Hello, I am Mr. Carter. I will be asking the trivia questions. Get your pencils ready and I will start," he said. He had a dullish, Sinister. Smith kind of voice.

"I shall now START. Question One; which three people invented dance music?"

Who invented dance music? How was Cara supposed to know! *I have no literal idea! Let me jog my memory! Hmm, I remember something about these two dudes, something about Chicago House or something? Oh, I remember something about Tess trying to remind me of someone's name by thinking of May. OH YES! Derrick May, Juan Atkin and Kevin Saunderson! Yes! It's a miracle!* Thought Cara and she quickly wrote down her answers.

"Question Two; Who sang the song, Ring of Fire?"

Ring of Fire, Ring of Fire. Cara tried to job her memory again and the something popped into her head.

Wait a minute. The first time we seen Chips dancing, just before we left, wasn't that one of the songs played? Didn't it say who sang it? Johnny Stash? Johnny Mash? Johnny Clash? OH YES!! LIGHTBULB MOMENT! Johnny Cash! Cara smiled as she wrote her answer, things were looking good so far!

"Question Three; what country and representor won Eurovision in 2017?"

Eurovision? That was a program they watched all the time! Cara knew the answer.

Cara wrote down her answer. *The answer is Portugal! And the representor is Salvador Sobral if I'm not wrong! Wow, these questions are getting easier and easier!*

But Cara was going to discover, this was not very true.

"Question Four; what is the different between arabesque and a la seconde?"

Huh? Cara had literally NO idea.

Umm maybe, arabesque is to the back and la seconde is to the front? I DON'T KNOW!! I'm just going to write that down.

So, again Cara wrote her answer (This time an answer she was not sure of). It was only a matter of minutes before you could hear Alfred's voice again.

"Question Five; What is a time step?"

Time step, time step, time step.

Hmm, sounds familiar, I remember Jess going all giggly to me and saying, 'Heeehee! Time step is-' ugh! It is either hop, flap, flap, step stomp or shuffle hop shuffle change! Well hop flap sounds a bit silly yet shuffle hop seems more sensible and still something Jess would giggle about! I'm going with that! Cara thought before, you know by now, wrote down her answer.

Few seconds later Alfred's voice came again. They hardly have any time, that's how much pressure it is.

"Question Six; What type of dance do you use the barre in?"

Barre? This was Ballet of course! Ballet and Ballroom are practically Chips' *life*. She always told her agents a few ballet facts every now and then. Writing her answer, Cara smiled, maybe this wasn't that hard!

Looking confident, she waited for the next question, it wasn't long after.

"Question Seven; who sang 'Hey Jude'?"

Hey Jude? Never heard of it! WHAT AM I GOING TO DO?! Who could it be? I've literal no idea, I'm just going to guess John Lennon! Cara, you should definitely know by now, wrote down her answer, not so confidently this time. She looked up to see Nice Creamy looking VERY confident. Clickoo looked alright, not THAT bothered.

"Question Eight; who sang Billie Jean?"

Billie Jean? This was the work of good old Michael Jackson!

See Creamy and Clickoo face, I know answers TOO! She thought as she wrote down her answer *confidently.*

"Question Nine; What is the Number One song of all time?"

Umm, didn't that change like, every year or something? Were they talking about in 2017? 2018? 2019? 2020? 2021? Could be any!

I'm just going to guess Flowers, as I feel that is kind of popular nowadays. Thought Cara.

Looking up again she saw Nice Creamy *and* Clickoo look confident. *GULP* she gulped.

"Last question, Question Ten; which country/city invented Irish Dancing?"

Ah! A lovely easy question to finish with! Ireland is the answer, in case it is not obvious enough.

"RIGHTY HOO!" came Felix's big loud voice. "TIME'S UP! Our Mini ALBERT EINSTEIN will be checking your answers now! Results on who won first, second and third place will be TOLD in FIVE MINUTES!" said Felix. He wondered off with Alfred.

"Umm, well, err- good lucks guys," said Cara, breaking the very quiet silence.

"Thanks, Crabbo Brain," said Nice Creamy, winking.

"HUH? How do you know I, err, like crabs?"

"Well Red Potatoes and Ravens and West Coast aren't *really* enemies, were friends-ish. So maybe I was interested to know things about our allies and found that out," laughed Nice Creamy, "Emma," she said lifting her hand for one of them to shake.

"Noah," said the boy as he shook her hand.

"Cara, as I, err - predict you already know,"

"I most certainly do!" she chuckled, "If I'm being honest, I'm kind of glad *we* got into the final, I think we deserve it!"

"I agree, I found that trivia pretty hard though!" said Noah.

"Yeah, I guarantee I got most wrong!" agreed Cara.

"Apart from the last question. It was literally SOOOOO easy!" laughed Emma.

"Yeah!" said Cara and Noah.

Then Felix and Alfred came back into the room, holding three pieces of paper.

"RESULTS ARE IN, FINALISTS! NOW, the amazing, fantastic number one, who gets THREE CLUES title goes tooooo …….." he did a dramatic pause, "EMMA MILLAR, NICE CREAMY, RAVENS!" said Felix as he gave

Emma three little pieces. "An amazing eight out of ten correct! Well done!!"

Emma shrieked with joy. "OMG! I CAN'T BELIEVE THIS!" she screamed as she took the three pieces! "YAY!" she added for extra effect.

"NOW, SECOND PLACE TITLE THAT GETS TWO CLUES, goes tooooo ……" more dramatic pause. "CARA MICHAELS, CRABBAY PATTAY, THE RED POTATOES!"

This time it was Cara's turn to jump and scream with happiness. She was so happy. Of course, she would have preferred winning first place, but second wasn't bad, better than nothing. She knew she'd get a few complaints from her team about not winning first, but she didn't care, she jumped and screamed and laughed and felt proud of herself, that was all that mattered.

"Congratulations!" said Felix as he handed Cara *her* two pieces, "A great six out of ten!" he added.

Cara looked at them;

I travel all around the world but stay on one corner. What am I?

And

Oooooh! Looks interesting, the others will definitely be impressed! Thought Cara. She stepped out of the studio/arena with Emma and Noah by her side. Noah was a bit bummed that he was third (four out of ten!) but was still a bit proud, and managed a few smiles.

Cara looked at her special crab watch (pink with white dots and a pink and white and blue crab in the middle) and saw the time. It was exactly eight o'clock. So, that means the *Chance To Dance* lasted the whole day. Cara was actually pretty pleased.

Words can't describe how pleased the others were. As soon as she walked into the tight, narrow corridor room, the others squealed and screamed. Some were screaming things, some were whispering 'Omg!' 'Omg!' over and over again, while others jumped down to hug Cara.

"Tell us, EVERYTHING!" said Jack after they had finished congratulating and hugging Cara. They settled down onto Chips' and Sinister. Smith's big, fat bed and Dave got them all a hot-chocolate (from the staff room).

"Well, it was interesting, very interesting," said Cara, sipping her hot chocolate.

"INTERESTING?? Give us DETAIL girl!" shouted Frank.

"Yeah! Tell us about the TRIVIA!" said Andrew.

"Alright, alright! Calm your crabs. I'll tell you!" Cara waited until they settled again. "OK, now, you want to know about the trivia, let's get started," exaggerated Cara, it was probably a two-minute story, but Cara was acting as if it would take at least thirty minutes.

"Now, he started with, like, the first two or three questions and I was feeling calm at first, because they were easy questions and I knew the answers. But then things started changing and it got harder-,"

"Ya! We saw your face! You looked worried at times and confident at times!" chirped Jess. She had finished her hot chocolate and had marks around her lips.

"-Yes, now, every one or two questions, they'd start to either get harder or easier. It was basically going, easy, hard, easy, hard.

"Even though, at every single question my heart was beating like never before. I'd chat to myself and think, heart still beating like crazy. And after I wrote my answer, the pressure slowed, but soon came back at the next question," continued Cara, finishing the last of her hot chocolate. She choked on the last marshmallow.

"Well, you're here now, and you've done a great job!" said Chips, giving her a beaming smile. Sinister. Smith nodded and clapped.

"Yeah. I'll have to thank Chips and Tess and Jess for some of those!"

Chips and Tess nodded and smiled. Jess bowed.

"Show us the clues then, eh?" said Mia.

"Oh yes, sorry I forgot." She read them out loud and suddenly Tess burst with excitement.

"OH MY GOD! THIS MAKES SENSE! Chips and I took a little trip to the library, because we were meant to go there days ago, because my riddle led there. When we arrived, we looked through books and shelves and everything, until Chips found a book with a note in it. It said '**POST OFFICE**'. Which is the same thing as Mia's clue, the riddle's answer is Post Office too, Chips and I looked in the Post Office but couldn't find anything. But *your* riddle's answer is Stamp, and I could have sworn I seen a section in the post office that said STAMPS!" squealed Tess excitedly.

"Oh my! This makes sense alright! Good job, young Tess!" said Jack and Chips agreed with him.

"We shall head down to the Post Office again tomorrow, yes Tess?" Chips asked and Tess nodded.

Cara suddenly lay down on the bed. "Ah! What a day!" she said.

"The day's over, tomorrow's a new one though!" said Harry and the rest agreed with him.

"Yes, we've done amazing though, here's to us!" Leo said, and they all lifted their hot chocolate mugs for 'cheers'.

15
ROB CREST

Days and days passed with not much luck. Apart from the 'S' and 'H' they found, they weren't doing amazing.

One day (day thirty-four to be precise!) Jess was in the tunnel 'searching'. Since the day on The Chance To Dance when they found the clues connected, they looked around the Stamps area in the Post Office and found a note that said 'RANDOM SKULL' but nothing else.

So, back to the point, Jess was wondering around the tunnel, until she came across this very peculiar man. He was leaning on a wall and was smoking a cigarette. He had shaggy, black hair and strange eyes. Eyes that looked blue and green and brown and black all at the same time. There was a pistol in his pocket, but he didn't even bother to take it out, even when he saw Jess. He just continued smoking the cigarette like a tasty treat.

"You, there! What's your name?" she asked, trying to sound like a true agent.

"Rob," he said simply.

"Rob what?"

"Rob Crest,"

"And you, Rob Crest, who do you work for?"

"Nobody,"

"Stop lying,"

"I am not." He said coldly.

"Then why are you here?" trying very, very hard to sound like a responsible teenager and not a stupid kid.

He sighed. "*Be-cause* I'm one of those people that are just here for a job. You offer me to work for you, give me a good salary and shelter, then it's a deal," he answered.

"Oh OK,"

"Yes,"

"Have you found a job yet?"

Rob stared at her. "No, I just said, I work for nobody,"

"Right, I knew dat,"

"Of course."

"Would you like a job?"

He frowned, "Well if I get one, I get one,"

"So you would. To buy more cigarettes," she said knowingly.

"Yes, especially these special ones," he said, taking it out of his mouth and examining it.

"OK. Do you have any Jammie Dodgers?" she put on her normal, babyish voice.

"No, but I do have these Jammie Dodger Flavoured Cigarettes,"

"Wow, I didn't know that was a thing!" Jess said, she looked at it, hoping he'd offer her one.

"They are,"

"Soooooooo,"

"Mm?" he obviously wasn't getting the message.

"Can I have one?" she asked, putting her puppy eyes on.

"OK. Try one,"

"Will day rot my lungs?"

"No, they are made out of Jammie Dodgers," Rob had to stop himself from saying 'you dumbhead'.

"Oooh, I feel so grown-up and sophisticated!" she said excitedly, taking the cigarette.

"Umm, yeah," he coughed.

"Sorry, I already am," said Jess, swinging her pigtails. She took a blow.

"Ooh! These are great!"

Rob nodded. "The Jams are getting really popular. Especially in cigarettes,"

"Rob – I mean, Mr. Crest, I want to make a deal with you,"

Rob tried to not look excited. "Yes?"

"If I give you a job, will you give me more Jammie Dodger Cigarette thingies?"

"OK. I need to meet your manager and we have to discuss my salary and stuff,"

"Oh ure. All the boring discussion stuff. Chips is still in the Safe Zone,"

Rob looked at her as if she was mad, "Chips, she's our manager boss thingy." Jess said. "Her name's unknown," she added.

"Right then, lead the way," said Rob uncertainly. Jess was pretty dumb and babyish looking (and acting), so Rob found it hard to believe this person was a human and not a plate of chips.

"YAY! I mean, of course," said Jess, still attempting to sound grown-up. There was no point.

She led him through the Safe Zone corridors, until they found The Red Potatoes.

"So, you're the Red Potatoes," he said, looking at the sign.

"Yup. Ever heard of us?" she said, proudly.

"Well, yes,"

"Great then, come on in!" she led them through the mini corridor before arriving at the beds.

Sinister. Smith and Chips and Frank were still there. They looked up to see Jess and a mysterious stranger.

"Excuse me," said Chips, taking out her gun, "I'll thank you to get out. Right now," she said in an icy tone.

"DON'T WOWWY CHIPS! Rob is only here for a job! I offered him to work for us. He's actually a pretty good assassin and agent!" Jess explained. Though, how would she know?

"Is this true?" asked Chips, looking at Rob.

Rob nodded, balls of sweat dripping from his forehead. "Yes, I came across this young girl and she offered me to work for you. Chips?" he said nervously.

"You should've just said! Oh, this is great my boy! Us Red Potatoes need more agents! Some are too young, or too ancient and computery like good, old Mr. Smith!" said Chips excitedly. "What's the name and age then?" she asked.

"Rob Crest, aged twenty-six," he answered, much more relaxed.

"Well, well then! What salary market are you looking for?" asked Chips, going in quickly. She wanted to finish the discussion a bit quickly so they could get down to some REAL business.

"Around fifty thousand pounds," said Rob casually.

"Deal!" said Chips, shaking his hand. She actually didn't care even if he wanted a million, she got paid a fortune by the government.

"Hey! How is that fair? He gets fifty grand while you mumble us with just one hundred pounds!" complained Frank, he had watched the whole conversation.

"Yeah!" agreed Jess, even if she didn't even care and continued smoking.

Rob laughed at Frank's comment, "I'm going to enjoy getting to know you all!" he chuckled. Tarnation

"WAIT A MINUTE NOT A SECOND! JESSICA LUCY BADGER! WHY IN THE NAME OF TARNATION ARE YOU SMOKING?! YOU'RE ONLY TEN! SURELY YOU KNOW YOU ARE NOT ALLOWED TO SMOKE!?" yelled Chips.

"Sorry, sorry Chips that is my fault. I gave her one. They are Jammie Dodger Flavoured Cigarettes," said Rob, truthfully.

"Jammie Dodger Flavoured? Oh, well, doesn't seem harmful," sniffed Chips. In truth, she was surprised.

"Ya, trust me Chips, day are so good!"

"OK, OK whatever. Mr. Smith, would you care to call the rest of the team using the watches you got?"

"Of course," said Sinister. Smith, he made a group call. Jess's candy heaven watch rang, Frank's **'KILLER BOY'** watch rang, Cara's crab watch rang, Mia's special karate watch rang, Andrew's alien watch rang, Harry's sock watch rang, Tess's 'kindness' watch rang, Leo's rock and roll watch rang, Chips' blood watch rang, and even Dave's and Jack's casual brown watches rang (while they were in the staff room enjoying a cup of tea and a biscuit).

"We must get you one of these watchies!" said Chips.

"Come to the Safe Zone immediately, I repeat, come to the safe zone immediately," said Sinister. Smith. Minutes later, the children (and adults) started pouring in.

When everyone was in Chips said, "OK, everybody, listen carefully. Rob is going to start working for us, he is going to tell us a bit about himself," nodding in Rob's direction.

Rob looked surprised. "I am?"

Chips glared at him. "Ahem, yes he is!"

Rob cleared his voice, "Oh yes. Hello everybody. I am Rob Crest, and I will start working for your agency, The Red Potatoes. I am twenty-six years old and have one brother; his name is Ron. Ron Crest. We were always mischievous, little boys. Instead of being the Ronald and Robert our parents always wanted us to be, we were Ron and Rob. My favourite childhood meal was spaghetti bolognaise and I never liked McDonalds.

"As a child, I always dreamed of being a superhero and turning the world into a better place. When I was in my teens, I wanted to be a plumber. But somehow, I became an agent. I use to work for Skull Stews, but then they got shut down. I was placed here, hoping I'd get another job and salary. Those Jammie Dodger Flavoured Cigarettes don't buy themselves you know!

"And so, one lucky day, today actually, a little girl-"

"IM NOT LITTLE!!" shouted Jess.

"-sorry, sorry, a GIRL, came up to me and we had a chat. She offered me to work for The Red Potatoes. I agreed almost immediately. It's not every day I get offered to work for one of the best agencies in the world! And so there you are," Finished Rob, he sat on the bed waiting for someone to say something.

"Lovely! Now, does anyone have any questions for Rob?" said Chips.

Mia put her hand up. "Yes?" said Rob pointing at her.

"Why do you hate McDonalds?" she asked.

"Well, Firstly I hate the name. It sounds like a cheap puppet show or something. Secondly, the food. Disgusting. Utterly disgusting. Especially those yellow sticks they call 'fries'," he answered, shivering at the thought.

Mia was stunned. Andrew put his hand up. "Mm?" said Rob, nodding at him.

"What football team do you support?" he asked, crossing his fingers.

Rob laughed. "I may get a few boos here but anyway, Chelsea,"

"BOOOOO! LIVERPOOL!"

"MAN U FOR LIFE!"

"BOOO CHELSEA THEY ARE JUST SOME STUPIED WEE!"

"MAN U IS BETTER!"

"GO ARSENAL! BOO CHELSEA!"

"LIVERPOOL!"

"SHUT UP!" screamed Chips. They fell silent. "Much better, next question."

Harry put his hand up. "Yes?" asked Rob.

"Did your parents ever make a fuss about socks being everywhere?" he asked.

Rob laughed some more. "I was never a tidy man, and yes, they complained that I needed to put my socks in the sock drawer, not the toilet," he said.

"WOW! Same-same!" exclaimed Harry.

Rob smiled. He quite liked these people. He soon knew everybody's name.

"So, Rob," started Chips. "We are going out again soon. There is a particular task I want you to complete,"

"Go on,"

"I need you to assassinate Keira Patterson, former spy-assassin who works for The Globs."

"What?!"

"You heard me,"

"I did but-"

"You work for me now, if you want that fifty-thousand-pound salary then you'll do as I say,"

"Yes Chips," said Rob meekly.

"ASSASSINATE? Isn't that a bit harsh?" whispered Tess to Andrew.

"I know right!?" he whispered back.

"Mr. Smith has located her and she is now in the Killing Kitchen. I want you to go stealthily and kill her. I've had enough of her," said Chips.

"If you say so, ma'am,"

"Now, girls and boys, you should all head off now," added Chips. "Off you go now!"

"Yes Chips," they all droned, before disappearing into the darkness again.

16
A SKULL IN THE
RANDOM ROOM

Everybody went out, Chips, Sinister. Smith, Jack, Dave and everybody.

Rob went straight to the Killing Kitchen to go find this Keira Patterson. He called it 'Operation Keira in the Killing Kitchen'.

Harry and Jess and Leo and Andrew decided to 'team up' and work together. They went through a corridor that leads to the Killing Kitchen. Simone had put a new sign that said;

THE KILLING KITCHEN
(IF YOU DESTORY THIS SIGN YOU WILL GET SUED BY THE GREAT SIMONE!)

"I love the fact she never gives up," remarked Leo.

"Mm," Agreed Andrew, deep in thoughts.

They walked and walked and walked some more. The corridors were getting narrower and narrower. Soon it was so pitch black they couldn't see an absolute thing. It was very silent too.

"Guys I think we went in TOO deep," whined Jess.

"It's alright, I collected a candle and some matches. I'll try and make this work," said Leo.

In a matter of seconds, a flicker of light appeared from the candle. They could see again.

"Phew! Thanks Leo," said Harry.

"No problem," came Leo's dry reply. Even if they could see, it was still scary and frightening.

They walked on and on, convinced something would be hiding in the darkness, it was very silent you could hear a pin drop.

CRACK a crunchy crack noise was heard, as if someone walked on a stick. Somebody was there. Somebody was following them.

"Hello?" whispered Andrew.

No reply.

Silence.

"I think I saw something," whispered Jess.

With a blow, Leo's candle was blown out.

GULP they all gulped.

"It may have been the wind or something," said Harry, unconvincingly.

Footsteps.

But they sounded as if they were going the other direction. Back to where they came from.

"Umm, what just happened?" asked Leo.

"It's dark again," whimpered Jess.

"I have more matches," said Leo. Sure enough, a minute later, the familiar flicker of light came again.

"OK. Let's continue our journey, I'm one hundred and ten percent sure there is something here. Or else, why did they make this area?" pointed out Andrew. His point made sense.

Soon, they found lots of ancient-looking rooms.

Jess read some of the titles. "The Sweets Room, Pool of Pringles, Death Combs, The Dragon Emporium, Great Rivers Like Never Before? What *is* this place?"

A few more steps later, they came across yet another room. The door was the same style and the lettering the same, but something about the room urged them to go in, maybe a clue was hiding in there. The sign read;

The Random Room

There was something written in tiny letters, so tiny, they couldn't even read it. But they had a small feeling, it wasn't one of Simone's extra comments.

"I have a feeling we've found what we are looking for," said Harry, "Something about this room says 'Go in Right Now if You Want to Win'."

"I have the same feeling," said Andrew.

"Same," Leo and Jess both chirped.

"So shall we go in?" asked Harry.

"I think we should," said Leo,

"Yeah," said Andrew.

Jess looked unsure. But they went in anyway.

Andrew opened the ancient door, it creaked as he did, and then a streak of light blinded them. The room was filled with lights.

"Woah!" exclaimed Leo, looking at the chandeliers and light bulbs and lanterns.

The Random Room, indeed was like its name, it was so random! There were; toy unicorns eating fake honey, dogs on unicycles, teddies playing chess, zebras on computers. There was even a toilet where an American High Doll was riding a blueberry!

"This is so random," Leo said, looking at the fairies playing football.

In an area there was a group of mangoes sitting together. They were watching a boxing match. It was a flamingo versus an elephant.

"This is random alright!" cried out Jess, looking at a pile of jewelry with a cornflakes box on top.

Every single place you looked, there was a wonder to look at. This room was anything but dull. This would be a child's dream room.

There were also beds with chicken eggs on them, tigers with hats on, cookies on washing lines, balls with bees balancing on them, mermaids sitting on chairs made of Sellotape and anything you could possibly imagine.

When they eventually reached the end of the room. There were still more wonders on the walls and floors. But something stood out in the middle of the wall. It was a skull.

It was so noticeable. If you looked at the wall, it would be the first thing you'd notice. If you tried to look past it, you wouldn't be able too. It was just so noticeable. So *real.*

Harry was the first to spot it. He gasped.

"What's wrong?" asked Leo. He saw the skull. He couldn't possibly miss it.

Jess and Andrew turned around too. They saw it. Alarm bells rang in their minds. Something about the skull was so familiar, so *close*.

"WHAT IS DAT?!" exclaimed Jess, the skull frightened the life out of her.

Andrew's mind was racing. This was a big jigsaw. And it felt as he had found the most important piece.

"GUYS, this all makes very clear sense! Remember the answer to Mia's riddle was Post Office? And that Tess found the words Post Office in the library too? And Cara's riddle answer was Stamp? And in the Stamps room, there was the words RANDOM SKULL? It all makes sense guys! It means in the RANDOM room, there is a SKULL. So, the skull must mean something!" said Andrew breathlessly.

"Jeepers, you are so right!" said Jess.

"This makes sense!" exclaimed Leo.

Harry was doing something on his watch.

"OK, I've tracked this place down. Anytime I need to, it can give me the directions to where it is. Because I have a feeling this place has an important part to play!"

"Good job Harry! And very good job Andrew," said Jess.

"Thank you," bowed Harry.

"Now, guys, us much as I am happy that we found this and all, this area tickles my spine. I recommend we ran back, tell the others and then we can *all* come back here," said Leo, shivering.

"I agree," said Andrew.

"Glad you feel the same!" said Jess.

141

"Sounds like a plan!" Harry said.

"Great, now let's skid-addle!" Leo exclaimed and they ran out as fast as they possibly could.

17
UNLOCKED MYSTERY

They arrived at The Safe Zone after a good twenty minutes later. Unluckily, nobody was there. Leo looked at his watch. It was 11:27am. So, there was still a good amount of time left.

"They've left me no choice but to make a group call," said Leo, pressing 'GROUP CALL'.

All the watches rang and soon after, they were all there.

Jess explained what they seen, describing everything so perfectly. From the noises to the lights to the random stuff and of course, to the skull.

"-It just stood there in the middle of the wall, staring at us, but the connection makes sense. It is a definite clue," finished Jess, sounding serious.

"Hmm, this makes very good sense," said Jack. He looked at his watch. "The day's not over yet, we have time to investigate this area," he said. Before adding, "Oh, by the way, I found these three letters laying in the middle of the floor. Must of fell out of some pocket. But I'm glad I found them," he said, showing them the letters; 'M', 'I' and 'V'.

"Wow, were getting REALLY close to finish these letter things. Only sixteen remaining" remarked Dave.

"Yup," agreed Tess, counting the amount they already had in her head.

Harry led them towards the area, using his watch. There was no spooky human sounds or footsteps this time. Or candle-blowers.

Thirty-minutes later they were standing in front of the familiar door they seen an hour ago;

The Random Room

"Woahhhh," they were all dazzled by the lights alone. Imagine their faces when they saw the stuff.

"OH MY!!!!" exclaimed Chips.

"WOWZERS!" said Frank.

"Amazing," whispered Tess.

"So cool!" said Mia.

"Impossible!" muttered Jack.

"Gracious!" Dave said.

"CRABTASTIC!" screamed Cara.

Chips was the slowest. She was busy admiring all the stuff. She especially likes the monkeys eating Jam, the ice-skating cats and the plushie chips riding tanks.

The fastest was probably Frank. He was so desperate to look at the skull, it may give him a brainstorm.

But, of course, he couldn't HELP stopping every two seconds to look at something. He specifically liked the toy bugs on kinder bars, the Easter eggs riding dinosaurs and the tanks on top of raisin towers.

Cara and Tess both loved the pandas on toasters, the crabs wearing elf hats and the tomatoes riding Egyptian Pharaohs.

Mia fell in love with the penguins swimming in popcorn, the robot giving out cakes and bakes and the brown creature thing that was snoring in bed.

Dave and Jack especially admired the minion reading *Jolly Men Plus Spurs,* the chihuahua playing the violin and the pencils in snow globes.

Which is *your* favourite? Is it the gingerbread men on pogo sticks? The snowmen lighting a fire? The lego-action figure swimming in a chocolate-cake a hundred times its size? The pretty dolls riding trains? The cowboys/girls grilling strawberries? The tank dancing with the tree? The choir of hamsters? The spoon playing tag with the plate? The giraffe eating a moon made out of cheese? The Princess Cat who lives in a palace made entirely out of burgers? The medicine-pill riding a roller-coaster? There's so much to see in The Random Room. I could have spent a whole day there, looking at all the creative and extraordinary wonders. It was to die for.

But The Red Potatoes weren't here to die. Or grill strawberries for the matter. They were here to *win*.

They arrived at the end of the long room and saw the skull. Of course, they did, you couldn't miss it. Even if you close your eyes, you would still be able to see it. It was so noticeable, so ugly, so *frightening,* so *spine-tickling.*

"Aha! Jack pot!" said Jack, "This, is the skull you are talking about?" he asked, even if he already knew the answer.

"Yes, what else?" answered Jess.

Sinister. Smith thought for a second, the skull, the whole point of this room was it. The sign written in tiny letters *had* to be about it. But what was it? What did it say? Skull here? Clues Hide? Riches To Be

145

Found? He was going to find out. He was going to impress the rest of the team.

"I know what may have the answer," he said suddenly, showing no emotion. "The sign written in tiny letters; I have a magnifying glass here. I may be able to find it out," he said, showing no enthusiasm.

"NO WAY STEVEN! THIS IS THE KEY TO THE RICHES!" shouted Chips dramatically.

He led them back outside and Leo lit a candle for him. He took out his magnifying glass and turned to the letters. They started getting

bigger

bigger

bigger

bigger.

Until he could just see what it said.

The riches are close. Skull holds the mystery.

"Umm, it says here, the riches are close. Skull holds the mystery," said Sinister. Smith casually, as if it was no big deal.

"SAY WHAT??" shrieked Frank, Leo, Harry, Andrew, Mia, Jess, Cara and Tess.

"REALLY???" exclaimed Jack and Dave.

"NO WAY! STEVEN HAS DONE IT AGAIN! TO THE RICHES!!!" shouted Chips. Words can't describe how happy and excited she was.

"Umm, Chips, what do you mean by 'to the riches?'" asked Frank, confused.

"What I mean lad is that, now that we know the skull holds the riches, it will only be a matter of time before we find those riches. What day even is it? Thirty-five? Thirty-four? If we find the riches quickly, we'll be known as the Smartest Agency in the World!" exclaimed Chips.

"Ooh, I like the sound of that," said Harry and they all laughed.

"Exactly! We need to find those riches quickly! We can't wait till tomorrow, as you never know, another agency might come along and find this, we better start our investigation now," said Chips.

"That is a good idea Chips," said Jack, "I think we should see our letters, maybe it may spell something useful out, even if we haven't found them all yet," he continued.

They looked. They had an 'E' and 'T' and 'H' and 'S' and 'K' and 'V' and 'I' and 'M'.

"Hmm," Frank thought out loud.

"Tim Keshv?" guessed Andrew.

"This EVMK?" wondered Cara, "It stands for Equipment Vehicles for Money Kidnappers," she added.

"Them is kv- I don't know," sighed Tess.

"Kit Shev?" said Frank.

"Kim Vets?" thought Mia.

"Sit Eh Vmk?" was Jess's guess.

"Those are very imaginative guesses children, but I have a feeling we need a bit more letters to work it out!" laughed Dave.

"I agree," nodded Jack

"But — but there MUST be a way to find those riches or discover something TODAY!" said Chips, frantic.

"You mustn't fret yourself, Chips. What we have found so far is great. Now we must go and search for more letters," said Jack.

"Yeah, I think so to," yawned Frank. "This is probably going to be a lot of work and I really don't feel like doing this at the moment." he added.

"Agreed,"

"Yup,"

"Same here,"

"ARROGANT, LAZY CHILDREN YOU ARE!" grumbled Chips, but all the same, sighed and agreed.

They headed back, and on their way back, at the corner of her eye, Cara saw a dark, gloomy figure. She heard their quiet footsteps. When she blinked, they were gone.

"Hey Mia," she whispered, "Is it just me, or does it always feel like were being followed?"

Mia stared at her. "Well, there was a time when it felt like somebody was behind me, but that was the only time. Why?"

"Oh nothing," Cara decided to keep the information to herself.

The rest of the walk was silent. No footsteps. And certainly, no dark figures.

18
POEMS

Mia went off. After they arrived at the main tunnel area, everyone went their separate ways. Frank and Harry went together though.

She was in desperate mode. They needed to find those letters. It was the key to winning the whole thing. She looked at her watch. It read 6:05pm. In less than two hours, the day was up.

She held her pistol close to her chest and walked cautiously. She looked for trails, people and clues. Unfortunately, most people had already headed back to their safe zones. It seemed like the clues did the same.

Not *everybody*.

After minutes of impatience, Mia finally saw somebody. A man. He was standing in the darkness, but Mia could still see him quite clearly. He was very tall, about six feet. He had shaggy blonde hair and pale skin. One could say he was pretty handsome. From the back at least.

"Hey, you! Long, dark, figure thingy, LOOK HERE!" Mia shouted. The figure turned around, almost too quickly. He stared at Mia. He had an interesting face. He had blue eyes and thin lips. And a broken nose.

He sighed as if the sight of a child annoyed him. It probably did.

"Look, kid, what do you want from me?" he obviously didn't know kids could be agents to, "I don't have time for this, go back to where you came from, you're not supposed to be here," he explained.

Mia grinned slyly. This was going to be interesting. "Oh, I'm very sorry, sir. I must have got lost and accidently bumped into you. Apologies, you, stupid dummy," she answered.

He raised his eyebrows, "In what way are you suggesting that I am stupid and dumb?" he asked, coldly.

"I'm not suggesting, I'm *saying.* You have no idea that children can also be spies, do you? How stupid, and you look like you've been in the agency world of years now," said Mia, nodding at wounds and cuts and his broken nose.

The man's temper began to rise. The girl was right, he had been stupid. He hated when he made a mistake.

He growled. "Indeed, I have, so I have better knowledge then you. I am older and wiser. You are just some pesky wee dirt,"

"Mm, like the others. Saying tiny insults to get the better of me. You've probably not even found a single sausage since day one!"

"My, my, I've got a spirited one here. Actually, I have found six riddles and seven letters. Though sadly, I have lost most of them. And some got stolen by agencies. Such as Marshmallow City and The Red Poetoes,"

"How much do you have left then?" asked Mia curiously.

"Two," he answered bluntly. "You're not getting any." He added for extra measure.

"I'll get to you!"

"And how do you plan that?" he said, icily.

"Easy-Peezy, ham and cheesy!" she returned.

"You're so silly, Mrs. Billy," he answered. Mia smiled. He was doing it.

"Go to the loo, Mr. Poo," came back Mia.

"You are fat, like a cat,"

"You're so sad, Mr. Bad,"

"Go kill yourself, you bad little elf,"

"Go and die, in the sky,"

"Egg and spoon, die on the moon,"

"Woof, meow, woof, meow, you're just an ugly cow,"

"You're a bean, not a queen,"

"Can you see, your wet wee?"

"Get a life, or a knife,"

"Don't hope or wish, you're just a goldfish,"

"Hey you're wonky, Mrs. Donkey!" Balls of sweat were started to appear on the man's forehead. He was running out of ideas. While Mia was firing ones at him like spitfires;

"Go and drown, under the ground,"

"You're in despair, you horrendous bear,"

"Ugly, fat, poo-poo, they all describe you-you,"

While he was trying to fire ones back;

"Umm? Read a book, no need to look,"

"Err – stay still, or pay a bill,"

"Eat — a pea, it's - err — it's not free,"

But he was doing very bad jobs of it. And eventually Mia beaten him with her spectacular skill of saying rhyming poems. He was embarrassed but also proud. He had never done a poem-battle, and surprisingly did pretty good. BUT he had been beaten by a child who was less than half his age. Pathetic.

"Give me them now, Mr. Seal, we made a deal!" said Mia, purposely making it rhyme to make him cringe.

The man shook his head. "What deal?" he asked slyly.

"You know what I mean, hurry up I'm keen,"

"Hmm, actually, I don't remember shaking on any deal,"

"Stop now, stupid cow!"

"What deal?"

"The deal, give it now or I'll make you my meal,"

"STOP THE RHYMING!"

Mia smiled. "The deal first please, or I'll make you wheeze,"

"SHUT UP, WHAT DEAL??" He shouted even though he knew what she was talking about.

"Time's running out, hurry or I'll shout,"

"THERE WAS NO DEAL!!"

"What do you choose, win or lose?"

"WIN!"

"Win means give me, lose means you WILL give me the hard way. The deal now, I don't have all day," Mia answered. She wanted something to rhyme so she did 'way' and 'day'.

"STOP IT! WE NEVER MADE A DEAL!"

"Last chance, or you'll dance," she said.

"DANCE??"

"Dance the hard way. You want to stay?"

The rhyming was totally driving this man mad. He had enough of rhyming poems to last him a century. "UGH fine! Here you go!" he said handing over the clues.

"Merci, you may go and pee!" Mia smiled and ran off towards the safe zone.

I bet I left you utterly confused. "What deal?" I hear you ask. Well then, my dear, I shall explain it to you. As you are not used to the spy world.

If anybody in the world of spying says to someone "I'll get to you!" that basically means that I am going to do something that will make you give it. And as Mia's next sentence was rhyming, so the man knew this was a rhyming competition.

If someone started their next sentence as 'Witches Watch White Whales,' it means they are doing a competition that you only say things starting with 'W'. (You may come across that in this book or other ones). So, there you go, I bet your spy knowledge is getting better and better as you read this!

Mia arrived seconds later and went in. She barely even looked at the clues herself, she was in such a rush.

Cara and Jess and Andrew and Frank and Jack and Dave and Chips and Rob were there. They all looked pretty happy. Maybe Rob actually succeeded in his mission to kill Keira.

"Hey Chips! I have some clues here!" said Mia.

Chips looked at her. "Really? Great then child! Show us,"

"I haven't looked at them myself," she replied as she took them out her pocket.

They said,

L. W. T. S.
(LUCKY DIP)
And

"Lucky dip?" asked Jess as she looked over Chips' shoulder.

"Ah yes, lucky dips are when you get more than one letter on a paper," answered Jack.

"How do you know that?" asked Rob. He felt a little bit behind when he was near this agency.

"Where do you think I was when we came back? At the secret office of course! I also discovered that there is four T's, four E's and three L's! So, we are so close to winning now!"

"Wow, but how did you not know that before?" asked Andrew.

"Because I have a feeling a member of staff comes there occasionally and puts some clues in there,"

"This is a miracle!" exclaimed Dave, "We only need four more letters!" he said as the rest of the team walked in. Leo and Harry looked tired.

"We were so close to getting a clue!" said Harry, explaining how they lost a roast battle against five Glob boys.

"Never mind, looks like Jack and Mia have got us a jackpot. Four left now!" said Cara.

Everybody smiled as Simone walked in with hot chocolate for them all. "With whipped cream and marshmallows!" she said. They all laughed.

They settled in as it had turned eight o'clock. They lay in the covers sipping their sweet drinks.

"Guys," began Mia. "I think I have a hidden talent for saying poems …."

19
FIGHT

The Red Potatoes' hope was starting to drift. Today was day forty-two. A whole week since they last got a clue. At least not a good clue. They found the four T's and L's and E's and stuff, so no help there. Even Jack couldn't find anything at the secret office place.

They went back to The Random Room, but nothing helped. It was the same random stuff and the skull. They tried hitting the skull, but nothing worked. They gave up and went back.

Dave suggested they look at all the letters and see what they could come out with. But it still wasn't working, they needed *all* the letters.

Though it was very impressive, they had twenty-two clues and there were twenty-five agencies here, some agencies had no letters to speak of.

Chips gave up looking one evening and went to the Safe Zone. She got a piece of paper and started writing all the things she'd do with the money. It wrote;

- Buy a yacht, a helicopter, a private jet, a designer toilet, a new set of jewelry and Arsenal.
- Give a bit to Frank, Leo, Andrew, Harry, Mia, Jessica, Cara and Tess. Because they did help after all.
- Same with Jack and Dave. Give them the few diamonds and two rubies they wanted.

- Give some to Chocolate World. We are friends and always help each other!
- Burn some. Oh, and film yourself burning them. You will look popular and of course, so rich you have to much money and need to burn some.
- Buy the whole Sports Direct
- Pay people to kill themselves. Works on dummies.
- Pay the government to make a new rule where jokes about bottoms and farts are BANNED.
- Take a bath in pound notes. Maybe not in jewels, as that may be terribly sore
- Enjoy the rest of the valuables and money.

(I do not agree with eight)

Anyway, where was I? Oh, I remember now, telling you how TERRIBLY the Terrible Group have done.

Every evening, they'd come back from an unsuccessful night and sip endless cups of hot chocolate before they fall asleep. This caused them to wake up lazily and tiredly. And made them in a TERRIBLE mood for the rest of the day.

Until, on day forty-two, their luck changed. They woke up usually, tired and moody, and had their muesli. Some of them didn't have an appetite and ate nothing. The same with Chips. She just drank black coffee, while, on the other hand, Sinister. Smith would eat keenly. Bowl after bowl after bowl. He finished a whole packet himself.

Jack and Dave met them minutes later, no different than the previous days.

They, too, looked tired and lazy. Like they all lost their spirit. Even jolly *Dave* wasn't himself lately. Which upset the rest of the team.

"Morning everybody, another day today, eh? Our luck will get better, I promise," yawned Jack unconvincingly. Though surprisingly he was right.

They decided to go out as a group. All of them. Even the adults. Chips, Rob, Sinister. Smith, Jack, Dave. Simone came for a bit.

"Have you been hanging out wiv the Poetoes?" asked Jess.

Simone made a look. "Sadly, Mr. Lewis asked me to go around *every* agency, so, yes, I have been with the Poetoes, but don't worry, I didn't even talk to Pamela," she answered. This was true. When Pamela tried to talk to her or say 'Hi Si!', she'd ignore her, or shake her hand in the air like a fly was bothering her. Pamela was discovered to be crying in bed because of this.

"Ha, serve that Wallsie Ballsie right!" laughed Jess. Simone left soon after that.

They went out, and started walking cautiously. They walked for minutes and minutes. Those minutes soon turned into hours.

"Ugh, this is hopeless," moaned Mia. Frank called her Moaning Mia.

"Shut up," she said, whacking him on the head.

They finally approached a door. It said;

FIGHTS FOR WINS
(COME AND FIGHT FOR A WIN)

"Fights For Wins?" read Andrew, "Uh, cool?"

"Did Simone write this??" asked Frank.

"No," Dave replied. "It's not her handwriting,"

"I'm guessing that whoever wrote this isn't allowed out. Like one of those staff that aren't S.Hs," said Harry. Everybody agreed.

"Should we go in?" asked Jess.

"Yes, we should. Our luck hasn't been good lately and this room might change that," replied Rob.

"OK!" the rest of them said.

Dave opened the door. It revealed a very interesting room. There was some kind of scanner on the ceiling that went green as it scanned. The walls were blue, a nice, darkish shade of blue. There were pictures on the walls, some looked like famous boxers, while others were just paintings of flowers or cottages.

In the middle was a ring, where boxers fight. Inside the ring was The Red Poetoes. There was Mac Hart (Chips' enemy), the S.H.M Matthew Holmes (Jack's enemy. Staff have enemies to you know), the S.H.A Miranda Grimes (Dave's enemy. Which seemed weird, as Dave liked everyone. Apart from Miranda, as she always made fun of him), Alex Walters (Sinister. Smith's enemy), Darren Young (Rob's enemy. They both were placed in the tunnel, hoping for a job. They fought over who would get one first), Lila Hart (Mia's enemy), Pamela Walls (Jess's enemy), Theo Turners (Frank's enemy), Lucinda Green (Tess's enemy), Greg Mills (Leo's enemy), Kenneth Loafer (Andrew's enemy), Samantha Hollister (Cara's enemy) and Jamie Williams (Harry's enemy).

Tess gasped. What were their biggest enemies doing here? And WHY them? Was this a coincidence?

They stood, big smirks on their faces. It seemed impossible, were they actually real? They looked like a vision, standing lifelessly, haunting The Red Potatoes.

"What is this?" whispered Jess.

"I have a feeling we are going to have to fight for a win. AKA, means we may get a clue if we win the fight," Andrew explained.

"Oh, Andrew, you're a genius! Of course, how did I not think of that?" exclaimed Jack.

"When will you decide whether you come onto the ring, or melt away like a coward?" said Mac. He had a harsh, cold voice, as if it wasn't even real.

Chips went red. She didn't want to look like a coward. Especially not in front of her biggest enemies.

"Come on, Potatoes. We have some people to destroy," said Chips as she walked into the other side of the ring. The others followed her.

Each member stood and faced their enemy. Frank facing Theo, Tess facing Lucinda, Leo facing Greg, and so on.

The ring divided into groups. There was a mini ring for Chips and Mac, Miranda and Dave, and the rest. The ring, as you guessed, is for fighting. Like in boxing matches. The Red Potatoes were going to have to fight their deadliest enemies for a win. For a clue. For the riches.

All the Red Poetoes, stood, smiling. Smirking. They all spoke at the same time;

"Remember the time I won against you in a fight, Leo?" asked Greg, slyly.

161

"Remember the time, when we were both five, I tripped you up and you doll fell in a massive, muddy puddle?" asked Pamela, slyly.

"Remember the time I tricked you into thinking there was an earthquake? You embarrassed yourself so much!" said Jamie, slyly.

"Remember the time, I kicked you so hard, you cried like a baby?" asked Samantha, slyly.

"Remember the time you were bragging about how cool you were, and I scared you with a monster outfit, and you screamed 'Mummy!'" asked Theo, slyly.

"Remember the time, you came to attack me, but tripped over a plate of chips?" asked Mac, slyly.

"Remember the time, I tricked you into falling into a smelly dustbin, and everybody was laughing so hard?" asked Lila, slyly.

"Remember the time, I scared you so much and you wet your pants?" asked Lucinda, slyly.

"Remember the 'ime I tripped ya up 'nd ya 'ace 'ell on a 'late o' spaghetti?" asked Matthew, slyly.

"Remember the time, I patted your back and then pushed you hard into a wall?" asked Miranda, slyly.

"Remember the time you were so mad at me, you lunged towards me, but I dodged and you fell on the floor?" asked Kenneth, slyly.

"Remember the time, I got the job to work for Skull Stews first and you said you would get it first?" asked Darren, slyly.

The Red Potatoes did remember. These were terrible memories they tried badly to forget. All those times The Red Poetoes made a fool of them or embarrassed them. Remembering them was hell. Losing a fight Leo was so convinced he was going to win, falling and dropping her precious doll in the muddy puddle, saying how brave he was, then got scared and screamed 'Mummy!' and embarrassed himself, wetting her pants in front of everyone, just because Lucinda gave her a fright. These were the worse memories ever.

Remembering them brought tears to some of their eyes. Some went red, some cringed and shivered, some closed their eyes. These monstrous, ruthless Poetoes had brought back memories they tried to forget. They must pay.

The Red Potatoes each ran towards their enemy. As if by some coincidence, The Red Poetoes all dodged at the exact same time. They all laughed spitefully as the Red Potatoes fell.

"You're such a loser, aren't ya, Frank?"

"Can't even move on two clean feet! Can you, Mia?"

"Once a loser, always a loser. You should know that Andrew,"

"Oh, look, it's the stupid Cara show! And she's got NO VIEWERS!"

The Red Potatoes go back up again, and tried again. Some ran again, some side-kicked, some punched, some lunged. But it was no use, The Red Poetoes always dodged.

It was as if it was some kind of game. The Red Potatoes attack, The Red Poetoes dodge, they laugh, say spiteful things, remind them about bad memories. This went on for a long time, before Tess put two and two together.

When Lucinda was standing, smirking at Tess, waiting for the attack, like the rest of Poetoes. Something came into Tess's mind. This was round thirty-seven of trying to attack The Red Poetoes.

Tess looked at Lucinda. She looked *faded,* as if she wasn't real. She looked at the other Poetoes. They looked the same, and they were all standing in the exact same position.

Tess looked back and the past forty-five minutes. The spiteful words the Red Poetoes said. The way they all dodged. The way they were bringing back awful memories. This made *sense.*

"GUYS!" shrieked Tess. The rest of The Red Potatoes, stopped and looked at Tess. The Red Poetoes just stood, facing their enemy, arms folded.

"This is all just a vision! That scanner up there, scanned us to see who our deadliest enemies are, then made them appear in the ring. They are here to make us lose hope, bring back bad memories, make us feel *useless,*"

"Richard Lewis probably wanted to test us, see if we can deal with our enemies, beating us, winning us. They are purposely bringing back these memories, Richard Lewis wanted to see if we were up for this, we need to outsmart these pesky, spiteful visions!

Just look at them, standing, same position, they aren't even looking at me! They probably can't even hear us! We need to outsmart them by coming by a different angle, or a way they won't feel us coming. Come on Potatoes, let's show Richard Lewis we can do this!" she finished.

The Red Potatoes cheered, while the visions stood. This made much more sense.

Frank used a grapple gun and shot himself to the ceiling. Then jumped right back at Theo, landing right on top of him.

"GO AWAY YOU, STUPID VISION!!" he shouted.

Theo looked at him. "You're still a loser Frank, nobody likes you, and nobody ever will," he said coldly.

"SHUT UP!" he said punching him with all his might. Theo looked lifeless, but still alive.

Jess threw a teddy bear at Pamela. Pamela dodged what she thought was Jess, because whoever created this vision, made them move when they felt the vibration of movement.

Pamela stared at the teddy bear and Jess sneaked up to her and attacked her from the back, making them fall.

"TAKE THAT YOU PATHETIC SIMONE-STEALER-SNOTTY-COW-DIRTY-PIG-UGLY-POOP!" shouted Jess, using her red boots to kick Pamela's sickly face.

Pamela said, "Get off, and go cry for your poor muddy dolly,"

"YOU ASKED FOR IT!" Jess yelled, and kicked harder and harder.

Dave pretend-ran towards Miranda. She felt him coming and dodged, yet this time Dave was ready for her. Instead of falling on the floor, Dave lunged sideways onto Miranda, flooring her.

"Poor, little Dave. Or should I say, big, massive oversized Dave?" laughed Miranda. "Loser!"

"Shut up Ugly McBugly, your days of being spiteful are OVER!" shouted Dave.

"Worthless garbage! Nobody likes you!" said Miranda.

"SHUT YER CAKE 'OLE!" Dave shouted and started punching harder.

This was the same with the rest of the team. They all out smarted the visions and attacked them. They punched and kicked until the visions started to fade away.

"YOU LOSERR . . ."

"YOUR USELESS . . ."

"NOBODY LIKES YOU . . ." they all said before fading away completely.

"WE DID IT!" they all exclaimed.

"WE OUTSMARTED THOSE VISIONS!"

"WE WON THE FIGHT!"

"WE'RE HEROES!"

The ring disappeared altogether, and the Red Potatoes went to greet one and other.

A random box appeared from the floor. It opened up and two single letters was written on a piece of paper, on black leather.

Chips went towards it and lifted it, showing a rather bright black letter, shining on the paper. It was;

"Woo-hoo! Another two clues for us!" exclaimed Mia.

"Now we only need ONE letter. This feels like a PIECE OF CAKE!" said Frank.

Cara was looking at all the letters that Jack had just taken out of his pocket. There was a word that stood out-

"GUYS, LOOK! The skull DEFINITELY has something to do with this, because those letters spell out the word SKULL!" shouted Cara, pointing at the 'S' and 'K' and 'U' and 'L' and 'L.

"Uh – good thinking Cara, but we already knew that . . ." mumbled Jack.

"Rude!" Cara muttered. Honestly, some people didn't appreciate anything!

They walked back to the Safe Zone as Simone insisted that they had done enough work.

"Very well," Chips said. She pulled a face. "The children may get a bit careless and make mistakes,"

"Thanks for saving our skins, Simone. I'm tired I could fall asleep for five whole years!" exaggerated Harry. Though that may be possible!

Simone got them hot chocolate with marshmallows and whipped cream and they settled down. It was only four o'clock.

"Let's play a game!" cried Jess.

"Jessica," frowned Chips, "Surely you are old enough to not play games anymore. And you should know that Mr. Smith, Simone, Jack, Dave and I are too old for silly games,"

"Yeah, but this is *different.* The game is called 'Make Up a Word' and whoever makes up the best word, wins!" Jess explained.

"If I'm being honest, that does sound pretty fun!" said Simone.

"I agree!" agreed Dave.

"Sounds nice," said Jack. Sinister. Smith nodded.

Chips frowned. "Fine," she muttered.

"Oldest to youngest!" shouted Mia. "Chips, you go first. You look like an oldie,"

"Ahem! Excuse your manners Mia Badger or I WILL ground you!" said Chips. "Will you believe it, Sinis - err – Mr. Smith is actually older than me!"

"Well then, Sinister. Smith, you go first,"

Sinister. Smith looked up and said, "Grufflypuffs,"

"Interesting word! Now move on,"

"Sofuishy," said Chips.

"Moranga," said Jack.

"Loo-woo-lingu!" said Dave. The room exploded with laugher. Mainly because the way Dave said it. Some hot chocolate spilled out of the cups. And some spilled out of noses.

"RedPoetoesAreRubbish!" said Simone. This caused some more laughter. And more marshmallows and hot chocolate coming out of noses.

"Chikkles!" said Frank.

"Flonga!" said Mia.

"Heeeeeeeeeeeeeeeeeeeeeeeeeeeeeeeeek!" said Harry. There was more laughter because the way he said it.

"Fleepx!" said Cara.

"Jkungo!" said Andrew.

"Mippity!" said Tess.

"Honkodonkowornysornywordlybirdlyblipblop!" said Jess. The room was an absolute mess now. Wet marshmallows and hot chocolate stains were all over the room now.

"I think Jess won!" giggled Tess.

"I agree!"

"Same!"

"Totally!"

"No doubt!"

Jess beamed with pride. It wasn't everyday somebody appreciated her funny skills.

20
WHERE IS
EVERYTHING?

More days passed. What happened on the fight day was like some kind of dream. It was all back to normal. Looking but not finding.

One day (day fifty to be precise), Jack suggested they all go out together. "We achieve more," he said.

Some protested bitterly. They wanted to achieve on their *own*. But Jack wasn't having any of it.

"To be a successful agency, you need to know how to work as a **TEAM**," he said, "So we're going out together. Whether you like it or not,"

So, they got dressed and had some muesli before going out. But as soon as they set outside, they saw something UNUSUAL. Outside was full of cobwebs and it was even darker, not a single candle in sight. In the distance they heard singing.

Here they come! Here they come!
Winners, winners, on the run.
Will they win the day away?
Will they lose the week's stay?
Mysteries, mysteries wait for them,
Will they find the precious gem?

"Some thing's not right ....." said Frank. Indeed, he was right. This was the first day this had ever happened.

"Hmm, weird. Maybe this one of those things Mr. Lewis doesn't tell us about for a reason," said Dave to Jack.

"Yeah, you might be right," he replied.

They walked on and on. There were more cobwebs and the singing was getting clearer.

"How come this ALL happened overnight?" asked Cara after twenty minutes. It confused the rest of them, too.

Something was extra unusual. The doors that use to be there, like Safe Zones, Pro Rooms and other rooms, just *weren't* there. Since it was so dark, they hardly noticed until they decided to go to the Dying Room. Which they couldn't find.

"Huh? Where is everything?" they all asked.

"Something is *definitely* not right!" insisted Frank.

Jack scratched his head. This also confused him. Was Lewis up to something? Or was this all a dream?

They walked on in silence. Determined to find *something,* that would help them. But nothing. They walked on and on, in the dark corridors and passage ways. Into nothingness.

This is until they came across a dark, wooden door. The only door they came across the whole day. It was jet black and it had cobwebs on its sides. In the middle, there was a skull.

The Red Potatoes stared. Was this what they had been waiting for this whole entire time?

Nobody said a word. But it was obvious what they were all thinking. Leo knocked on the wooden door.

It opened. Steam came out like fire ashes, exploding into their faces. They coughed and swatted it away.

"Should we go in?" whispered Tess as they all stared inside the room. The only thing they could see was darkness.

"You go first," Mia nudged Jack.

Jack took a deep breath and went in. The others followed behind.

21
INSIDE

Crackles and chuckles were to be heard. Fire and dust were to be smelled. Darkness and more darkness were to be seen. A candle flickered on. It was on an ancient table that had knives and ammo and blood on it.

Another candle flickered on. And another, and another. All revealing a table with items on it. Behind every table was a picture. It had a human's face and some writing. Some said;

KENNY FISHER; AGENT OF THE DARK
FREYA ELIZABETH; KILLER WINNER
LORD FRANKS; RICH IN BLOOD
CONNER STEALTH; STEALTHILY WEALTHY
LILITH MORGAN; PLAYS A GOOD GAME
DONAL YOUNG; STARTER.

The Red Potatoes stared in awe. More candles began to flicker, revealing more and more pictures. When they nearly got to another door, one last candle flickered. It showed a picture, of a few faces.

RED POTATOES; NEAR TO VICTORY

"That's us!" somebody whispered. It indeed was. They all stared gasping, before something grabbed them into the next room.

They were pulled with a big force. They screamed and screamed, going through what looked like tunnels. Then, they started falling. Falling into darkness. Suddenly, they hit the ground. It felt like the end of a very long, ugly train journey.

When they got up, moaning in pain, they looked around. It was an interesting but quite empty room. The walls were made of ancient stone, the floor was hard wood and there were candles laid in rows beside the walls.

As they walked (silently), they looked at the portraits on the walls. The ones in this room were different from the ones in the first room. There were pictures of knights on horses, people fighting with swords, dark shadows holding guns, pictures of old paperwork.

When they came to the end of the room there was a wooden table with a crystal, glass ball on it. Above it there was yet another portrait. But one with a face they know very well. The title read;

RICHARD LEWIS; INHEIRITOR

Below, the ball glowed and a face appeared. It was Richard Lewis. Everybody gasped, as Lewis's pale face looked at them. He smiled. Then began to speak.

"Hello Red Potatoes. I have been waiting for this moment for fifty days now. The moment where one agency is this close to winning." He gestured with his fingers. "And that one agency, is YOU. You only need one more letter and you will win. The thing is, I have that letter. And to win it, you have to pass these challenges," and with that, his face disappeared.

Before anybody could say a single word, the walls began to open, leading to another corridor. Without saying anything, they all walked in.

22
KILL THE AGENT

After walking for a few seconds, they saw a sign half way through the room. It read;

~ KILL THE AGENT ~
(NO TALKING ALLOWED)

Just a few meters away stood away a man. They recognized him almost immediately. It was Will Scott. One of the best agents ever. It probably wasn't the real Will Scott, just a clone or vision. Their first challenge was to KILL Will Scott.

They were going to win this.

But, to do that, they were going to have to outsmart him. But they didn't have ten minutes to spare to think of a plan. They were going to work it out as they went through. Like Jack said, to be successful, you needed to work as a TEAM. Even if you're not allowed to talk.

There was a timer on one wall. That meant they only had a certain amount of time. It said 19:59. So the timer had already started and would ring in another twenty minutes. They had to move.

Frank decided to make the first move. He dashed towards Will at full speed. Leo and Mia followed behind.

As soon as Frank arrived, Will moved to the side and put out his leg. Frank tripped over and landed on the floor with a heavy THUD. Leo and Mia made their move quickly.

Mia cartwheeled over and tried to kick, while Leo went up from behind. Will dodged Mia's kick and turned around and punched Leo. Mia tried to attack again, but Will got hold of her leg and flung her away.

The rest of the team ran forward. Unsure on what they had to do, they just ran and did some random move. Or if somebody fell or got flung, they'd ran back like headless chickens.

This isn't working, we need a proper plan! Cara thought frantically. It had been ten minutes of non-stop flinging and falling and *failing.* They needed a plan.

And Cara had one.

She walked towards Will. Then, standing a good meter away from him, waited. She waited for her teammates to come and form a circle around Will. She hoped they did so.

Everybody stopped and stared at Cara. Including Will. They wondered what she was doing and why she was just standing doing nothing.

I don't get it! Thought Frank. Then he walked and stood beside Cara, thinking maybe she wanted back up.

Cara gave a thumbs-up sign and gestured for everyone else to come. Then using her finger, drew a circle in the air.

Now they understood.

Tess came walked to join the circle. Then Leo, then Harry, then Mia and Dave and Chips and Jack and Andrew and Jess.

After forming a circle around Will, Cara looked at Harry, who was exactly opposite her. She gestured for him to attack. So, he did.

He ran to Will and made his attack, but fell. Then Cara came running and attacked Will from the back. He fell. Oh, everybody thought, Cara wants us to attack in pairs so we confuse him.

Chips and Tess were next. They ran and ran around in full speed. Will got confused and didn't know where to look. In every direction he'd see someone rush pass.

Eventually he got dizzy and closed his eyes, and that's when they attacked. Tess gave him a boot in the bum and punched his stomach. Chips lifted him up, gave him a punch and threw him. That was their job done and dusted.

Next was Leo and Jess. They were going to confuse him, but in a different way. Jess stood behind Will and Leo was in front. Jess gave him a kick from the back, he turned around and prepared to kick. But then Leo kicked him from behind so he turned around and prepared a kick. But then Jess kicked him from behind so he turned around and prepared a kick. This went on for a minute, until Will was facing Leo and Jess came and ran on top of him. She was on his shoulders and kicked at his ears and face. He dropped to the floor. Leo and Jess joined the circle.

Up next was Andrew and Dave. They confused him, attacked him the made him fall.

After was Jack and Frank. Same thing. Confuse, attack, fall.

After everybody finished there go, Will just lay on the floor for a few seconds before disappearing completely. They cheered. They finished challenge one.

A big green sign with a green tick said 'GOOD JOB. CHALLENGE OVER'

Then, a door appeared out of nowhere. It was brown and wooden with a white skull on it.

"Anyone want to take the pleasure to open it?" asked Jack. Everybody shook their heads. Harry even shrieked 'YOU CAN JACK!' which made them laugh.

Jack opened the door that led them to their next challenge.

23
SKELETONS GALORE

Another sign met them as they walked into the dark room. It said;

~GET THE SKELTONS INTO THE FENCE AREA~

(LESS TALK, MORE WORK. OXEN MAY HELP. OH, BY THE WAY, IT'S GOING TO BE SKELETONS GALORE)

"Skeletons?" said Andrew. AND just as he said that about one thousand skeletons appeared. They were running wild. There was a large area surrounded by a fence. There were lots of different kinds of skeletons. There were big ones, and small ones, tall ones, short ones, handsome ones, ugly ones, dirty ones, clean ones, fancy ones, not fancy ones, nerdy ones, not nerdy ones.

"So, we have to get all those wild skeletons into there in twenty minutes?" asked Mia, looking at the timer and pointing at the fence area.

"Yeah, but look. I see lots of oxen over there. Maybe they could help us," said Dave.

"In what way?" asked Leo.

"We could ride them. Then we could lead the skeletons inside the fence area," explained Dave.

"That, is a very good idea," said Jess, in her most grown-up voice. She sounded a bit like Donald Trump. They all laughed.

They didn't feel like laughing a few minutes later. After each person had grabbed an ox, they began. So did the timer. They had twenty minutes to get every single skeleton inside the fence area.

There were only eleven oxen so Chips didn't get one. That was no problem at all, as Chips was as strong and scary as an ox.

Sinister. Smith seemed to be enjoying himself. He was near smiling at when nobody was looking or listening, he'd scream 'YEEHAAAA!' which was not very Sinister. Smithy.

But it was harder than they expected. Firstly, it felt as if the ox was about to fling each person every second. So, it made riding a lot harder. Secondly, the skeletons were VERY, VERY hard to catch! They were running and running in different directions. Thirdly, the fence door had to stay open, so occasionally the skeletons would run back out.

Frank tried to scare the skeletons towards the fence but it wasn't working.

Jess got so mad, that she jumped off her ox all together and landed on a skeleton and started punching it "YOU, STUPID, LITTLE, UGLY, THINGY!" she muttered punching it until it was nothing but crumbs.

"I'M AN ANGRY JESS WHO KILLS NAUGHTY SKELTONS," she screamed running like a maniac. But she didn't succeed.

Leo ran towards the fence, hoping they would follow him. Only one did, an old grandpa skeleton that was chasing after him because he was mad. Because Leo accidently knocked out his false teeth.

"WHERE'S MY TEETH??" it screamed.

There were lots of other methods they tried but nothing worked. The skeletons didn't go in and the number of skeletons seemed to have grown. It was skeletons galore!

Ten minutes left. Nine, eight, seven, SIX. Time was running out. Mia had an idea.

"OK, YOU'VE LEFT ME NO CHOICE BUT TO SHOUT!"

screamed Mia, "YOU BAD, BAD SKELETONS! YOU ARE DISOBEYING US! WE ARE OLDER AND WISER THAN YOU SO IF YOU DON'T SCUTTLE YERSELVES IN THERE, WE'LL WHIP YA AND KILL YA! SO, WHAT'S IT GOING TO BE?"

As soon as Mia spoke the skeletons froze and listened. When she finished, you could see the fear in the dark wholes of eyes they had. They immediately ran towards the fencing area, screaming. Here are some things they were saying;

"HELP! I WANT MY MUMMY!!"

"I'M TO YOUNG TO DIE!"

"THE HUMAN THINGIES ARE COMING!!"

"WE'RE GOING TO DIEEEEEEEEEEEEE!"

"I DON'T WANT TO DIE!"

"Has anyone seen my teeth?"

Eventually they were all squeezed inside the fence area. Jess closed the door.

"Good riddance!" she muttered, closing it with all her might.

"YES! FINALLY! Thanks Mia! Great job!" said Tess. Who was kind and never forgot to thank people. Even if it was threatening a bunch of skeletons.

Another green sign appeared. 'WELL DONE. CHALLENGE OVER.' It read.

"Well, we've finished challenge two so let's see what our NEXT challenge is going to be. Instead of looking back," said Frank.

"Someone sounds jealous! It's obvious you wished YOU could have saved the day. It's okay Frank, we still appreciate ya!" teased Cara, "Not!" she added.

"Me? Jealous? Of MIA? Nonsense girl, you're talking rubbish," he said, going red. Everyone laughed.

"Next challenge guys!" said Andrew, as a door appeared.

"Anyone want to take the pleasures NOW?" asked Jack. Everybody just looked at him.

"YOU CAN JUST DO IT JACKIE!" said Harry in a funny voice. Everybody laughed some more.

Jack opened the door, it led, to the next challenge waiting for them.

24
FINDING IT

After they went in, they looked around the room. It was pretty filled. There were cupboards, closets, chest-of-drawers', boxes. Basically, lots of places for storage. The sign read;

~ FIND IT ~
(WHEN YOU SEE IT YOU'LL KNOW IT)

"Right. So, we have to find something we don't know what it is?" frowned Cara.

"Well, it must be something that stands out. That way if we see it, we'll know it's it. Like it says in the sign," Andrew pointed out.

"Yeah, good point mate," nodded Frank.

"I get it now!" said Jess.

"Well in that case, less talking, more finding! The timer has already started for thirty minutes this time!" said Mia.

So, they set off. Searching for the thing they had no idea what it is. They all started opening cupboards and closets. Quickly opening it, searching inside it, then closing it. That's all you could hear, the sound of closing closets. **BANG, BANG, BANG, BANG.**

After they finished the closets with no luck, they didn't fear, they started searching the drawers. Opening, closing, opening, closing, opening, closing.

"I FOUND SOMETHING!!" shrieked Harry. He took out a hammer.

"WOW A KEY!!" shouted Jess.

"Hammer," corrected Andrew.

"Something tells me it's not the thing we are looking for," said Dave.

"Why?" demanded Chips.

"Because, firstly, no sign appeared, secondly, why should one dusty old hammer be it? I certainly didn't think it was it when I saw it," explained Dave.

"Bad explanation," muttered Chips. But she knew he was right.

They continued searching the drawers. And when they finished, never fear, the boxes are here, they searched the boxes. This was everyone's thoughts while searching:

Mia: *why can't we just find the stupid thing and end this challenge?*

Jess: *Please can I find it, I WEALLY wanna look superb and cool!!!!!*

Cara: *Cara, queen of crabs, just find the thing and be over with it!*

Tess: *I hope I find it. I really want to be useful to my team and help.*

Frank: *IF I DON'T GET THIS I WILL LOOK LIKE A COMPLETE FOOL!!*

Leo: *Sooooooo boring.*

Andrew: *Ok Andrew. Find and win. Find and win, find and win.*

Harry: *I smell something very fishy. It smells like cabbages.*

Chips: *UGH. We haven't found it already. This team is so useless.*

Jack: *Search, search, search, search, search, search.*

Dave: *when will we find it?*

After what felt like endless boxes. They eventually finished every single drawer, closet and box. But nothing. Not an interesting thing whatsoever.

"Maybe we should DOUBLE check things again. We did search quite quickly, so maybe we missed something," Cara said, pointing to the timer that said 23:36.

SO, they searched once more. Taking a little bit more time to look around what was inside. As soon as they finished the cupboards they moved on to the drawers. Then the boxes.

But still nothing. Not a sausage. Or a crumb. Or a clue what the thing might be. The only thing they had was a hammer.

"This isn't working," whined Mia.

"Neither is whining nor moaning," snapped Chips.

"OK guys," said Andrew, "This isn't working, is it? So, we need a new plan. I bet Lewis didn't put the thing in the closets and boxes,"

"Then why are they here?" asked Tess.

"Because he wants to *trick* us. If we see cupboards and things that's the first place we'd look.

But that's the point. He's trying to see if we are smart. He's outsmarted us. The thing is somewhere else in the room. And the hammer is a clue," Andrew explained.

"Good explanation," muttered Chips.

"So we need to think OUTSIDE the box," he said. "Let's start now! Look under things, check for secret compartments, destroy the walls for all I care, WE need to find it, only ten minutes left!"

"Good point Andrew!" said Rob, enthusiastically.

So, that's exactly what they did. Some people looked under closets and boxes just in case, other looked at the walls to see if there was a button or secret compartment there, others checked the floorboards. And one odd thing they spotted was that there was one floorboard a sort of different shade as the others.

But, after what felt like endless hours, they gave up. They couldn't find ANYTHING.

"UGH. So much for having a GOOD plan!" said Frank.

"Humph!"

"Ugh!"

"Why can't we just find it!?"

They tried searching some more. But nothing. Jess used the hammer to knock the walls, but nothing. Eventually she got so, so, SO mad this is what happened.

Jess was standing on the odd floorboard when this happened. She was holding the hammer. And she was **MEGA MAD.**

"I'VE. HAD. ENOUGH!!!!!!!!" she screamed. Hitting the floorboard with the hammer so hard it destroyed. And revealed a piece of shimmering diamond.

"OH MY GOD JESS!" exclaimed Cara, "Look!"

Chips walked towards the diamond and picked it up. It was sort of obvious that THIS was the thing they were looking for.

"YESSSSSSSS!!!! GOOD JOB JESSICA!!" she shouted.

"Jess!" Jess corrected.

"Good job Jess and Andrew!" cheered Leo.

"We just destroyed a floorboard!" screamed Jess.

"BOTHER THE FLIPPIN' FLOORBOARD JESS! WE FINISHED THE CHALLENGE!!" shouted Tess. For a girl who was kind and sweet, Tess DID have a bit of spirit and danger in her.

"Oh," said Jess, feeling a bit dumb. Rob gave her a Jammie Dodger flavoured cigarette as a reward.

Another green sign appeared. 'GOOD JOB. CHALLENGE OVER.' It read. Then, a door appeared.

"Anybody?" asked Jack. They just laughed. Jack sighed, but then laughed. Before opening the door to the next challenge.

25
SPY AND PIE

The door led to more rooms. As soon as they went in, there was a wall with eleven doors on it. They each had names above them. And a pie on it.

CARA MICHAELS
JESS BADGER
HARRY PETERS
LEO BROOKS

And so on and so on.

"Say whattt?" said Andrew. He was confused. So were the rest of them.

"Do we go in?" asked Tess, just the moment a sign appeared explaining the situation.

EACH PERSON MUST GO INSIDE THEIR ROOM. COLLECT THE PIE AT THE DOOR AND CARRY IT AS YOU GO. GO INSIDE THE ROOM AND SPY ON THE PEOPLE INSIDE. DO **NOT** MAKE A SOUND AND DO NOT BE SEEN. KILL THEM STEALTHILY AND MOVE ON UNTIL YOU GET TO THE END. CARRY THE PIE AT ALL TIMES. 40 MINUTES, YOUR TIMER STARTS NOW. BEGONE!

"That explains it," said Mia as they finished reading it.

"Yup," said Frank.

"Well, I guess this means we have to go collect those pies," said Jack. They each took the one at their door, and smelt it.

"Key Lime pie! My favourite!" said Cara dreamily.

"RASPBERRY! YUMMY!" shrieked Mia.

"Yes! Blueberry pie!!! Mmmmmm," said Jess, licking her lips.

"Strawberryyyyyyyyyyyy," said Harry, drooling.

"APPLE PIE! APPLE PIE! I LOVE APPLE PIE!!" sang Frank.

"Pumpkin pie! THIS IS A MIRACLE!" said Tess.

"CHERRY?? PIEE?? CHERRY PIE??? EEEEEEEEEEEEEK!" Andrew screamed like a girl; the others laughed.

"LEMON MERINGUE! Yes!" said Leo.

"Ooh, Shepard's pie!" said Chips, sniffing the pie with delight.

"Steak pie? Delicious!" said Dave.

"Pecan pie!" exclaimed Jack.

"Ooh, MEAT PIE!" said Rob.

"DO WE GET TO EAT THE PIES????" shrieked Andrew.

"No!" said Leo, shaking his head, "No, no, no! The sign said we have to CARRY the pie till the end. That is half the challenge. Can we resist our favourite pies? Are we tough and focused enough, to not be distracted by our favourite pies? Can we, do it?"

"YESSS!!!" they all screamed.

"OK, let's do this. Let's get in there, and SHOW Lewis what we are made of!" cheered Leo.

So, off they went. Holding their pies, they each opened their doors stealthily and slowly tip-toed in. The door shut gently behind them.

The first thing you'd notice about the room was its darkness. It was the darkest room you'd ever come across. Now, I know I've said that seven million times in this book, but this one is FOR REAL. Anyway, it was really dark. Each person's room was the same.

Just before they could look into the darkness some more, a door opened. At the exact same time for all of them.

A candle lit. Now they could see properly. They each peeked at the person from their hiding place, the person was the same for all of them. But, of course, they didn't know. Ignoring the smell of delicious blueberry/Shepard/Cherry/Apple/and whatever else pie, they examined the person carefully. It was a man. He had icey blue eyes, electric hair, army clothes and a candle. He put the candle on the table and looked at something else.

It was a map of the world.

Jess was too short to see it, so had to look up a bit more. Unfortunately, she carelessly made a vase fall. It was on the table she was hiding behind.

SCATTER, SCATTER, SCATTER.

The man turned around. The broken vase met his eyes. He took out a walkie talkie and said, 'Need back up, repeat, need back up!' then a blurry voice answered, 'Back up coming.' The man put the walkie-talkie back in his pocket, picked up the candle and walked towards the vase.

He put the candle on the table and kneeled down to examine the vase. He picked up a piece of glass. While looking at it, he smelt something. Something that smelt like Blueberry pie.

He stood up and followed the smell. Just he could come any closer, Jess grabbed the nearest rifle and hit him on the head quickly. He fell to the ground, knocked out.

Just then, the door opened again. This time, four men came in. For men and one dog. Jess nearly screamed.

One of them gasped as they spotted the knocked-out body. They rushed towards the man to see what happened. They saw the vase.

"Hmm," one said, "Maybe an accident happened?"

"Don't be ridiculous Mitchell! Does it LOOK like an accident to YOU?" grumbled the biggest one. He was probably the leader of the pack. Jess, Frank, Andrew, Leo, Mia, Cara, Andrew, Tess, Chips, Jack and Dave held their breath, hoping the dog wouldn't come any closer.

This was all part of Lewis's plan. Give them the same moment and see how each of them react. Seven of them knocked out the first man, one killed the man and three left him until back up came. So, for some of them, there was five men.

As for the vase, it fell on its own. The men and everyone were all robots. It was ALL part of Lewis's plan.

When all men examine the body (or vase) the dog sniffed the air. He smelt a pie. A raspberry pie in Mia's case. A key lime in Cara's case. A steak pie in Dave's case.

The dog moved towards the Red Potato in the room. Let's say it's Tess. As the dog moved closer and closer, Tess had a plan, she peeked up a little and blew out the candle. The men and dog looked up.

"Which one of you, nipple-sticks blew the blooming candle out?!" said the boss.

As The Red Potatoes have known each other for a long, long time, they sometimes think the same, have the same ideas. Another six did the exact same. They blew out the candle. But the others had another plan. They stealthily killed the dog with suppress ammo. So, nobody heard a thing. It was a risky plan, but at least the dog was off their hands.

Andrew was one of those people. He had killed the dog but he had four men left (one was knocked out).

After a minute a plan popped into his head. He quickly reached for one of his pockets, and took out a grenade. His heart started beating quickly. Should he do it? In his life he had never heard of a nearly twelve-year-old KILLING five men in one go. But after all, that was what his life. His career. A spy. A killer.

He threw the grenade towards the men. He moved a bit further away so he didn't get damaged. After a few seconds it exploded. Sending the men flying through the air.

Trying to avoid looking at the bodies, Andrew crept towards the door, to the next room.

Tess was doing the same. After she had blown the candle, and the man asked the other men the question, she had gone to action. She tip-toed towards the biggest man and snapped his neck. He landed with a big thump.

"Huh? What was that?" one of them asked. Since the candle had been lit out, they couldn't see anything. Plus, they were a bit thick, so even if they could see, it would take them a while to figure something out.

Tess walked on, it's like the pie had given her powers. As well as being delicious, it seemed like it had given Tess the power to see in the dark.

She stood behind another one. She snapped his neck. Another thump.

"Wha-what?" the same person asked. "Jeff? Jeff? JEFF. Speak Jeff!"

"Shut up Mitchell! You know very well we are not meant to call each other by our first names. Boss said so," replied the other man.

"I don't think Boss is here," gulped Mitchell.

"What do you mean?" demanded the man.

"He's not talking, I can't even hear him. Maybe something happened to him. Like Jeff," whimpered Mitchell.

"Walker! Call him by his surname,"

"Is that all you care about Bryant?"

While the two men were arguing (Tess had killed the dog and knocked out the first man), Tess walked up to Bryant and snapped his neck. *One left!* She thought.

THUMP. He fell to the ground. Once again, Tess heard Mitchell's whimpers.

"What was that? Carl – err - Bryant?" he gulped. Two seconds later he was on the ground. Tess had snapped his neck like the others.

"Well, that was amusing," she said as she crept to the door.

Tess and Andrew were not the only ones who moved on to the next room. The rest of the agency also finished from room one. Each of them used a spectacular idea to get rid of the men. Now they all moved on.

Mia cautiously opened the door. It led to some kind of factory room. There were machines, science lab things, lab coats, goggles and potions.

There was one man mixing potions, his back turned. *Phew! Only one man, this may be easier.* She thought. But she was wrong. The rooms were going to get harder and harder. Not easier.

This man had a sensitive nose he smelt the pie in no time. This was bad luck for Mia. And Leo and Frank and Cara and Chips and everyone else.

"I don't remember food being in the laboratory," he muttered. Walking in Mia's direction. They all wished they could just let go of the pie.

He arrived in Mia's hiding place and Mia jumped onto him. She snapped his neck. The others did the same, as they had nothing else to do.

After he landed on the floor, thin letters started appearing out of nowhere. They said;

DISGUISE YOURSELF AS THE LABORATORY MAN.

After they all read it, they did as it said. They took off their own clothes and wore the lab coat. They just fitted their shirts inside the pockets.

They moved on. They all killed, talked, used other disguises, trespassed without knowing, had to fight, and knock people out. As time went by things got harder. But they all managed to finish it in time (unharmed).

After they all opened the last door, they all greeted each other. They cheered and congratulated each other. After a few minutes, Harry shrieked "DO WE GET TO EAT THE PIES??" and after a few seconds of laughter a sign appeared that said LAST CHALLENGE COMPLETED. EAT THE PIES. SENDING YOU NOW.

Instead of overthinking what 'sending you now' meant, they all wolfed down their pies in seconds. "Yummy!" said Jess, and everyone murmured in agreement.

They sat down for a second to relax. "What a day!" said Frank just before everything went dark.

26
SHE'S BACK!

Light. Leo shook his head and sat up. He was back in the Safe Zone. Along with the rest of the Red Potatoes. Seconds later, Jess sat up. Then Mia, then Andrew, then Harry, and Dave and everyone else.

"What just happened?" said Dave. He looked around. Everyone looked as confused and dizzy as him. Apart from Chips. She was looking down at her leg. She picked something up, a little smile on her face, and showed the rest of the agency.

It was a black shimmery letter. The last one. It was

"OH, MY ACTUAL GOD!" shouted Mia. They all cheered and shrieked.

"TAKE OUT ALL THE LETTERS!" Tess shouted. Jack felt into his pocket and took out all the letters. He placed them beside each other and they looked at them carefully. They looked and looked and looked until their eyes watered. They couldn't see a sentence.

"Well, there is the word 'skull' and 'times' in there," said Cara.

"Oh, I see the words 'the' and 'on'. . ." said Harry.

"Guys, how about see what words we can find then write them all down on a piece of paper THEN try and work them all out?" suggested Tess.

"Good idea," said Jack, taking out a piece of paper and a pencil from his pocket. He wrote down 'skull' and 'times' and 'the' and 'on'. "Anything else?" he asked.

"OH! I see the word 'TAP'!" said Chips. Jack wrote it down.

"OK, what letters do we have left?" said Dave.

"E and V and T and E and L and W," Jess said.

"E and V and T and E and L and W. . ." muttered Mia. They all looked.

"FLOPSGASMACK!" Frank shouted, "The word is TWELVE,"

"Oh yes!" cried Cara. Jack wrote it down. He held the paper up.

"So, we've got, 'skull', 'times', 'on', 'the', 'tap' and 'twelve'," he said. They thought carefully.

"OH MY ACTUAL DIRTY SOCKS! The sentence is 'Tap on the skull twelve times!" Harry screamed. But it all made sense. The Random Room, The Skull, The Sentence.

"YES HARRY!!" They all cheered.

"LETS HEAD TO THE RANDOM ROOM SKULL NOW!" shouted Andrew. And they all shrieked back in agreement.

Harry's watch led them to the Random Room. And in ten minutes they arrived. If they hadn't been so excited and less focused, they would have noticed the long dark figure following them. It smiled to itself.

Jack quickly opened the door to The Random Room and they ran in, at full speed. They didn't even stop to look at the grilled strawberries or pogo-stick-riding-snowmen.

They reached the end of the room in no time. They caught their breath and Chips slowly walked towards the skull. She tapped on it. Once, twice, three times, four, five. Until twelve.

Nothing happened.

Then the ceiling opened and a staircase appeared. They gasped in astonishment.

"This is it; this is what we have been looking for," whispered Mia.

Chips slowly took the first step; the others followed her until they got to the top. It was a room. Not any room. It was filled with rubies and diamonds; emeralds and sapphires and ambers and gold and silver and golden coins and pound notes. There was a huge sack on one side of the room. But, in the middle, sitting on a golden chair was Richard Lewis. He was staring at them, smiling.

"Good job Jack and Dave. Looks like you've led your team to the riches!" he smiled. Jack and Dave's mouths just stayed wide open in shock. It was Jess that spoke first; "Wow," she said.

"Indeed, Little Jessica. A bulldozer will be coming now to put all the riches into the sack, then you will take it with you, home, back to your agency.

"I will leave you now, but the bulldozer will come soon. Enjoy the riches, Potatoes, you earned it!" he said before disappearing.

Before anyone could say a word, or indeed, even move, the door on the floor shut suddenly and a few lights went off. Then, smoke appeared. And after it all went, standing in the middle of a room was a face they had seen ages ago, but remembered it like yesterday.

It was the creepy-snack-handing-too-nice-airport-suit-wearing lady from the bus. The person that had been spying and following them for the whole time.

They all gasped in horror at the sight of her. I say 'they all' but not all of them did. Jack and Dave and Rob had no idea who she was, so stared at her, confused.

"Well, well, well. If it isn't the best spy agency in the world. Oh, that sounds wrong because they have not noticed me SPYING on them for fifty-two days," she said. Her voice was croaky and ugly. Not soft and sweet like on the bus.

"Who — who are you?" said Jack. His voice was wobbly.

"Oh, sweet little *Jackie* and *Davey* and *Robbie*. You may not have seen me before, but it is safe to say I have been serving some little **SNACKIES** to these rats," she pointed at the rest of the agency, "on a bus. So, they have seen me serving them, AND spying on them at the back of the bus," she said.

Suddenly Cara spoke, "It's true! She handed out snacks on the bus and I spotted her looking at us from the back of the bus. Every now and then I'd FEEL like I was being followed, and now I know WHY!" she said.

"YEAH, THOSE CRISPS TASTED REALLY OFF!" shouted Frank.

"Yes, it is true. I bet you are wondering what brings me here. Well, I work for a mad professor by the name of Professor Barnabas Oakslay. His laboratory is a shed. Or should I see UNDER a shed. From outside, it looks like a normal boring shed, but underneath, it's a whole new planet.

"Anyway, I and my employer work hard to make disgusting potions, curse people, and spy on people. But as we are greedy, we want to be RICH. We want money and gems and valuables, so when we heard about this event Lewis is holding, we knew this was our chance.

"So, Professor looked at his future-telling-snow-globe that tells up to sixty days of the future. And we saw that *you* won so we had to follow and spy on *you*. So here I am. Here to kill you and take the riches!" she finished. And took out a sword.

"Any last words, *peasants*?" she snarled.

"Yes," squeaked Jess, "What's your name?"

"Kristina Crawford. Or, I like to call myself Krissy Killer,"

"Anymore?" she smirked. "No? Well, next stop, the graveyard," she said as she ran up to them, clutching the sword.

When she nearly got to them, they all moved and fell onto the floor. She dropped the silver sword. Frank quickly went and grabbed the sword before she could stop him. She stood up.

"Give it back, child!" she said.

"That'll be £3.97 for you," he said pointed at her, "And £2.13 for you," he did a spin and pointed at her again.

The rest of the Red Potatoes were laughing their heads off. Especially Andrew.

"Don't you dare mock me!" she threatened. She did a few movements with her hands then sent a blasting wind at Frank. It made him fall off his feet. The sword landed on the floor, near Kristina, who picked it up and smirked.

Once again, she ran towards the rest of them, leaving poor Frank laying on the floor. She charged like a mad bull at full speed, they all dodged and tried to kick, but the end of the sword caught at Jess's finger, it started bleeding.

She cried out in pain and held at her bloody finger. This gave Kristina another opportunity, so she sent another howling gust of wind at Jess. She flew into the air before landing with a thump.

"Who's next?" said Kristina. She licked her lips, before charging again. They all screamed and dodged, but Mia stood and kicked Kristina in the stomach. She clutched her stomach for a few seconds before leaping back up again.

She headed towards Mia, but Mia ran away, which was bad news for Leo who was behind Mia.

"BLOODY NORA!" Leo shrieked as Kristina ran after him, quickly. She tried sending some wind at him but he dodged and ran in a different direction. She'd save him for later.

Suddenly, Tess started running up to Kristina, faster than she had every ran before. Then, she leaped and somersaulted onto her, flooring them.

The sword flung out of Kristina's grip and landed on the floor, a few centimeters away from Chips. Chips grabbed it and looked over at where Tess was punching Kristina. She ran forwards, but suddenly, another furious gust of wind came from Kristina's hands. It made Tess fly and reach the ceiling before falling to the ground.

Andrew and Mia were nearby when this happened, so they had been knocked off their feet, too. Dave, Jack, Rob, Chips, Leo, Harry, Cara and Sinister. Smith remained.

Kristina jumped back up again and looked at Chips' direction. She started doing more movements with her hand. Chips knew what was coming so dropped the sword and ran, screaming. But she wasn't quick enough. The wind, made her fly through the air too.

She started chasing after Dave and Jack who were running for their lives, Harry and Leo tried to think of a plan.

"How about we both go running then, like bowling balls hit her?" Harry suggested. Leo thought it was a good plan. So, it was set in action.

Harry and Leo started screaming as they ran towards Kristina. She turned around and stared at the in-coming boys. She held her sword, ready to rip them, but they hit her with a big force it sent her to the ground.

She got back up quick as quick and ran towards the boys. Her sword flew off somewhere else.

She kicked them high up like footballs. They landed with some more thuds and thumps.

Cara took hold of the knife and tip-toed towards Kristina. But she was chasing after Dave, who ran towards Cara, so, Kristina saw Cara. Cara screamed and dropped the knife.

Kristina grabbed it and smiled, happy to be reunited with her sword. She made more hand movements and sent a big, big, big gust of wind at Cara and Dave. They flew in the air like flying birds.

Jack watched this and gulped. He knew he was next. He tried thinking of a quick plan, but before he knew it, a big wind was heading towards him. THUD.

Rob looked worried. He had to do something. He started creeping up behind Kristina.

He suddenly attacked her from the back, making her fall. Her sword flew in the air before falling back. It was heading towards Rob's head. He immediately ran away.

Just as he was running, Krissy Killer (such a bad nickname!), made the hand movements. The wind hit Rob and sent him flying, like the others.

Sinister. Smith was last standing. To Kristina, he looked like he might be the easiest yet, but she was wrong. VERY wrong. She sent some wind at him, but he ducked, so he didn't get affected. She tried charging at him, but he dodged, she tried throwing the sword at him, but he avoided it.

Eventually she got so mad she was getting careless. One time, she dropped the sword and Sinister. Smith caught hold of it. She was standing right next to him, so he stabbed her in the heart. She screamed and started fading away like a vision.

27
HOME PARTY

Moments later, everybody started getting up. They cheered Sinister. Smith and a few seconds later, the bulldozer *and* Richard Lewis came.

"I'm back! What happened? You all look deathly pale!" he said.

"Don't worry about us, Mr. Lewis. Just happy!" said Rob.

"OK. It's great you found an agency to work with, Rob! Now. Let's get these richies into the sack!" he said.

After ten minutes or so, everything was in the sack. "We'll get it delivered to you know. You'll find it at your agency. Thank you for joining the competition and very well done on **wining**! You may go back home now," said Richard Lewis.

"WAIT!" shouted Tess, "What about Jack and Dave and Simone? Will they stay with us? It feels as if their part of our agency now!" she said and everybody nodded in agreement.

"Oh." said Lewis, "Well that decision is up to Jack and Dave and Simone,"

"Oh, I'd love to stay with you!" said Dave.

"Yeah, same here, I definitely want to work for the Red Potatoes!" said Jack.

"I'll go fetch Simone," said Lewis. Few minutes later, he and Simone were there.

"Oh, that sounds amazing! Yes, please one hundred and ten percent!" she said.

"OK everyone. Go pack your bags, I'll announce that you won and that the competition is over," Lewis said.

"Thank you, Mr. Lewis," Chips said, shaking his hand.

"YAS! THANKS SO MUCH! NOW I CAN FINALLY BUY A FLUFFY UNICORN!" exclaimed Jess, happily. Everyone else said thank you. Frank and Leo and Andrew and Harry even gave him a high five.

They all ran back from The Random Room back to their Safe Zone. They packed everything they had. And got ready for the announcement. It came soon.

"Please, I would like everybody to stop what they are doing NOW." There was a pause. "Now, I am here to announce that The Red Potatoes have won and FOUND the riches. So, the competition is OVER. Everybody must pack their bags and head out where the buses are waiting. NO KILLING OR ANYTHING AS YOU'RE GOING OUT. There are cameras, and whoever breaks that rule, will be killed. Happy Packing!" his voice disappeared.

"Off we go!" said Chips.

They headed out into what was dark. Lights have been put out everywhere to help people see where they are going. People gave The Red Potatoes death stares and side eyes as they were walking out. But they really didn't care. Who did care about what those weirdos think? They arrived outside, and saw Sam-Bus-Driver waiting.

"OMG, IT'S SAM!" shouted Cara. They had totally forgotten to breathe into the lovely fresh air they haven't seen in over fifty days because of Sam. They thought he *died.*

"Great to see you, Sam! We thought you were six feet underground!" said Chips.

"Nah, 'ot me. The 'eirdo woman, 'ocked me out, but 'idn't 'ill me!" said Sam. He gave all the children a smile and introduced himself to the newcomers. Jack, Dave, Simone and Rob.

When they sat down Dave said, "Now, I took a book out of The History Room, so now is the best time to read it, to get to know you all better!" He opened to 'Children' section. "Oooh! Check this out!" He said showing them the following pages;

NAME: FRANK JOHNSON
AGE: 12
PERSONALITY: FUNNY, ARROGANT, COOL
HOBBIES: FOOTBALL, SPYING, BEING COOL
FAVE FOOD: PIZZA
RATED IN GENERAL: 7/10

NAME: JESS BADGER
AGE: 10 1/2
PERSONALITY: FUNNY, WEIRD, INTERESTING
HOBBIES: GAELIC, PLAYING, BEING BABYISH
FAVE FOOD: JAMMY DODGERS
RATED IN GENERAL: 8/10

NAME: LEO BROOKS
AGE: 12
PERSONALITY: FUNNY, SMART, SPORTY
HOBBIES: STEALING BISCUITS, FOOTBALL, SPYING

FAV FOOD: SWEETS
RATED IN GENERAL: 7.5/10

And all the others.

After thirty minutes, they finally arrived back at the agency.

"Arrived home!" chirped Sam.

"Thanks mate," said Chips, handing him a tenner.

They all got off and Chips got the keys to inside. The rest of the agency had heard about them winning so as soon as they walked in, they all shrieked "*CONGRATULATIONS!*".

When I say 'they ALL' I mean they ALL! Every single person that works there greeted them. From Millie Mush, to Florence First Aid, to Alex Basil, to Love Texas, to Vicky (all of those people are adults).

"Thank you, thank you. Miss Mush, please prepare some special COOKIES AND CREAM, and let's party!!" said Chips.

"But Chips, who are they?" asked Becky from the good group, pointing to Jack, Dave, Simone and Rob.

"They are new agents; they are going to work for us. Oh wait, I believe the sack of goods arrived?" asked Chips.

"Ah yes!" said Vicky, "appeared out of nowhere in the living room!" she added.

"Great! **LET'S GET THIS PARTY STARTED!**" shouted Chips.

And that's what they did. They had jellies, pies, COOKIES AND CREAM, toffee apples, chocolate peanuts, red velvets, *Victoria Sponges,* cakes, chocolate chip cookies, fairy cakes, buns and any other yummy dessert you can think of!

They put on music, they dressed up however they liked, they brought toys, there was a live circus, they had games, there was **bingo** and Chips won twenty quid, there was bubble-blowing **elephants**, there was a **FUN FAIR** and there were a hundred other cool things.

"THIS IS THE BEST DAY OF MY LIFE!!!" they all screamed.

Everybody played together. There was party games, including Musical Dancing Statues, Eat, Eat, Eat!, Pass the Jess and lots more!

Chips, Dave, Jack, Rob, Frank, Leo, Andrew, Harry, Mia, Jess, Cara and Tess did a dance performance for them all.

They did K-Pop, *Ballroom,* **Rock and Roll,** *Line Dancing and Hip Hop.*

Everybody cheered and laughed at some of their clumsy attempts. It probably *was* the best day ever.

When they eventually got to bed (at 4:25am), The Terrible Group thought about their adventure. It was as exciting as scary. They couldn't wait for their next super spy adventure.

ABOUT THE AUTHOR

MENNAH ABDALQADER is the author and illustrator of the Red Potatoes books. She was eleven when she finished writing her first book (this one!) and has continued writing ever since!

She is a Muslim originally from Palestine, but has lived in the UK for most her childhood. She currently lives in Northern Ireland with her Mum, Dad and great brother Mohammed. She goes to Enniskillen Integrated Primary School and has lots of friends.

She likes dogs (she keeps begging her parents for one), reading, fun, playing football, and most importantly, eating sweets. Her favourite Red Potato character is Sinister. Smith (for his talent of being funny without even knowing it. Mennah has that talent too!).

She hopes you've enjoyed this book and will continue reading about The Red Potatoes. She rewards you with a Jammie Dodger for finishing the book. Don't let Jess see it!